Diary of a PARENT TRAINER

Diary of a Parent Trainer

yes, that means you!
learn to train your grown-up!

jenny smith

DELACORTE PRESS

Juv
Sm¡

Text copyright © 2011 by Jenny Smith
Cover art copyright © 2012 by Shutterstock

Delacorte Press is a registered trademark and the colophon is a trademark of Random House, Inc.

Visit us on the Web! randomhouse.com/kids

Educators and librarians, for a variety of teaching tools, visit us at randomhouse.com/teachers

Library of Congress Cataloging-in-Publication Data
Smith, Jenny (Jennifer Russell)
Diary of a parent trainer / Jenny Smith. — 1st ed.
p. cm.
Summary: Thirteen-year-old Katie Sutton, a self-proclaimed expert on grown-up behavior, begins writing a user's manual to help other teens train and operate their parents, but when her own mother starts dating Yellow Tie Man, Katie needs all of her expertise to get rid of him.
ISBN 978-0-385-74198-9 (hc) — ISBN 978-0-375-99035-9 (lib. bdg.) — ISBN 978-0-375-98894-3 (ebook)
[1. Mothers and daughters—Fiction. 2. Family life—England—Fiction. 3. Dating (Social customs)—Fiction. 4. Diaries—Fiction. 5. England—Fiction.]
I. Title.
PZ7.S651414Di 2012
[Fic]—dc23
2011024704

Book design by Heather Daugherty
Printed in the United States of America

10 9 8 7 6 5 4 3 2 1

First U.S. Edition

For my beautiful mum
With love and thanks
XXX

CONGRATULATIONS!

You are in possession of at least one Grown-Up. You have probably had your Grown-Up for some time, possibly all of your life. Now, at last, you can discover the skills you need to operate them successfully.

THIS EASY-TO-FOLLOW USER'S GUIDE WILL HELP YOU TO:

- achieve optimum performance from your Grown-Up or Grown-Ups
- undertake straightforward maintenance and repairs
- ensure smooth operation, in most situations.

! CAUTION

Your Grown-Up incorporates many complex modes and functions. Familiarization with these is essential before difficult maneuvers are attempted.

BEFORE USING YOUR GROWN-UP

Read this guide. It contains detailed information on the operation and care of your Grown-Up. Keep it safe and easy to access for future reference.

Tuesday, July 28: 4:23 p.m.

In case you're wondering what undiscovered genius is writing this User's Guide, it's me!

My name's Katie Sutton, I'm thirteen years old and I may, quite possibly, be one of the world's leading experts in Grown-Up behavior. For many years I've been studying their strange modes and functions.

I like to think of myself as a bit like the famous wildlife expert David Attenborough—only instead of studying chimps, hyenas and fruit bats, I'm studying my mum, my nan and my Auntie Julie!

My studies of them, and of other Grown-Ups I've encountered, have led me to write this excellent guide. After all, someone needs to . . . and who better than an expert on Grown-Up behavior like myself? You see, *it's a jungle out there*. One that's full of Grown-Ups. And according to the law of the jungle, you either eat or you get eaten. . . .

In this comprehensive guide, I'm going to share with you my secret knowledge of Grown-Ups, gained from years of intensive study and experimentation.

You too can become highly skilled at:

1) understanding their insane behavior

2) predicting their next moves

3) operating them to your best advantage.

With my help, I guarantee you can stay one step ahead of your Grown-Ups so you can survive their embarrassing weirdnesses. How cool is that?

You probably think an (as of yet) undiscovered genius and possible world expert should live somewhere interesting and stimulating—in a huge exciting city or, failing that, in any town big enough to have a shopping center. Unfortunately, I'm not so lucky. I live in Brindleton, voted the Most Boring Village in Oxfordshire in a recent survey (conducted by me).

Brindleton's not the quiet, pretty little village you might imagine it to be. It's a sprawling sort of a place that's a mixture of little cottages, posh detached redbrick houses and millions of public housing units—like the one I live in.

I live with my mum; my older sister, Mandy, who's fifteen; and my little brother, Jack, who's eight. Dad's no longer around. The final member of our family is Rascal. He's a West Highland terrier and he's twelve years old, which is *eighty-four* in human years! He's a small white scruffy bundle of a dog with hilarious pointy ears, and his main hobby is licking people's faces.

My enormous extended family also live in the village. For some reason *hardly anybody ever leaves*. Spooky but true. On one hand, it's great for research, but on the other, I can't walk down the street without being attacked by at least one auntie. I can't go to the town gardens, the park, the local shops . . . or *anywhere* without bumping into someone from my gene pool.

My nan (Mum's mum) works in the minimart. So I can't even go there without her sticking her very nosy nose in my business. Nothing's sacred, believe me.

Take this morning, for example. I went in to buy some ice cream. Nan Williams was grimly stacking toilet paper rolls into a huge pyramid. I tried to sneak past without her noticing me, but it was no good.

"I hear your brother's got **A BAD STOMACH!**" she shouted at full lung capacity, so that anyone within a five-kilometer radius could hear. "Your Auntie Susan told me. How's he doing; is he getting over it?"

"Yes," I whispered, my face burning hot.

"Messy business! How about you, Katie, have **YOU** got the runs?"

There is no such thing as privacy when you live in Brindleton.

Still, every cloud has a silver lining, as Nan would say. Being surrounded by so many Grown-Ups who think they have a right to broadcast the tragic details of my life and comment on everything I do is tough. But it's forced me to develop some vital skills and techniques—all of which I will share with you in this brilliantly useful guide.

USEFUL HINT

One way you can stop Grown-Ups figuring out your evil master plan for Grown-Up Domination is by covering this guide in brown paper and writing DIFFICULT MATH EQUATIONS on the front in permanent black marker. Your Grown-Up will be delighted and proud when they see you with your nose stuck in it.

This is exactly the sort of fantastic trick that gives you the advantage when dealing with Grown-Ups.

You might be wondering why you should believe a word I say, so I should probably tell you a bit more about myself. I'm just your average teenager. I'm five feet tall, with green eyes and straight, shoulder-length black hair, which just hangs round my ears in an uninteresting way. I think my chin is slightly too pointy, which is a family trait. Brindle-ton's full of people with pointy chins. And I have hideously skinny legs, which have been compared to Twiglets due to my knobbly knees.

Mum says I'm "striking-looking," which is her way of avoiding saying I'm not as beautiful as my cousin Hannah—who has long blond hair and the perfect nose—but Hannah is also my best friend in the whole world, so I don't mind.

My other best friend in the whole world is Louise, who we call Loops because she's got very curly red hair. Hannah and Loops are both totally amazing and fab in every way. They make me laugh so hard, stuff comes out of my nose.

But now it's time for a confession. Even though I may consider myself a world expert in operating Grown-Ups (which sounds a bit bigheaded, I have to admit), *I'm not always an expert at operating myself.*

I'm not very coordinated. Or as Hannah would put it, I'm massively clumsy. I'm always tripping on the school bus, or bumping into people when I'm hurrying to my next class and dropping my books all over the floor.

And now that I'm a teenager I regularly have "curse of the giant spot" days, when I have to hide my pointy chin or my nose or whichever part of my face is afflicted behind my homework folder.

Finally, there's my tendency to get myself into ridiculously embarrassing situations. For example, in my final year at elementary school I turned up in a costume for charity . . . *one week early*. I'm still majorly traumatized by the memory of myself in that clown costume—complete with revolving bow tie and giant shoes.

But that's nothing compared with the way I seem to embarrass myself when I'm around one particular person. When he's anywhere near me, I totally malfunction.

This is because I'm Officially in Love.

The lucky person (ha ha) is the unbearably, unbelievably gorgeous Ben Clayden, who doesn't know that I exist despite the fact that me and Hannah constantly stalk him around the village and school. Hannah's Officially in Love with him too, but we've agreed that in the—admittedly unlikely— event one of us gets him, the other will back off and become a bald, toothless nun who lives in the Himalayas.

BEN CLAYDEN: THE FACT FILE
- Three years above us in school
- Almost sixteen

- Lives in the posh end of the village because his parents are doctors
- The most attractive person in Brindleton, and possibly the world
- Brilliant at art. Probably better than Leonardo da Vinci or Picasso
- NOT RELATED TO US!!

That last point is a huge bonus, believe me—and quite possibly a miracle, considering our whole family lives here. Even if Ben Clayden had some hideous deformity we'd still have to consider him for procreation purposes because he's not a blood relation.

But he's not hideous—far from it. He's tall and athletic and has dark golden-blond hair and lovely eyes—the sort of deep blue you could get lost in. And his chin is not in the least bit pointy! If he went on *The X Factor,* he'd win even if he sang like a cat being strangled because all the girls, mums and grannies in the whole country would vote for him.

He's *so good-looking*! When I see him I start to hyper-ventilate. Sometimes, when we walk past him, Hannah has to remind me to breathe.

Being in love with Ben Clayden has ruined our lives. Nobody else can ever match up to his perfection.

For example, I used to have a thing with Thomas Finch. His mate Neil Parkhouse asked Hannah to ask me if I'd be Thomas's girlfriend and I said yes, but then *we never talked to each other*—how crazy is that? I know he liked me. One time in math he wrote my name on his arm with his ball-point pen.

Thomas Finch has lovely puppy-dog chocolate-brown eyes and messy chestnut-brown hair, but as he never said a word to me, the whole boyfriend thing was just too weird. I dumped him right before the summer holidays started.

It was cowardly how I did it:

ME: Hannah, will you tell Thomas Finch I'm not going out with him anymore?

HANNAH: No. Tell him yourself. It's not fair to get someone else to do it. If someone dumped me, I'd want them to do it themselves, not send a friend to do their dirty work!

ME: Loops, will you tell Thomas Finch I'm not going out with him anymore?

LOOPS: Okay.

(Loops goes up to Thomas Finch.)

LOOPS: Katie says she isn't going out with you anymore.

THOMAS FINCH: Oh.

Thomas hasn't spoken to me since (so no change there!). I haven't seen him for ages. I think he went to Spain on holiday.

Maybe I shouldn't have split up with Thomas. It's quite cool to have a boyfriend; it makes you look more popular. That sounds as if I never cared about him, which isn't true. In fact, I really did like Thomas, but he can't have liked me back much or he'd have found *something* to say to me. It's just my luck; I'm destined to be alone, bald and toothless. . . .

It's only a few weeks into the summer holidays, so I'm having the *best* time lazing around, writing this and not having to think about homework or teachers or my evil second cousin Leanne (my Archenemy).

Apart from living in Brindleton *and* having about a hundred relatives watching my every move *and* having freakishly skinny legs *and* **NOT** having Ben Clayden as my boyfriend and a few other things, things are pretty okay right now.

Life is sweet when you're in control.

Thursday, July 30: 2:20 p.m.

GETTING TO KNOW YOUR GROWN-UP

It is essential to become familiar with your model of Grown-Up before attempting to operate them. Make a note of their most common modes and routine functions and of any recurring problems.

Soon you will be able to anticipate most of their actions and take the necessary steps to ensure that they perform to your best advantage.

I just had to use that line: Getting to Know Your Grown-Up. Lots of operating guides use it: Getting to Know Your Tumble Dryer or Getting to Know Your Lawn Mower. But what are the manufacturers expecting? That you exchange life stories with your toaster and then take it out on a date? It's not a bad idea, actually, now that I think about it— you're guaranteed some delicious buttered toast at the end of the evening.

!REMINDER TO SELF:

Must start a website called dateyourtoaster.com.

The *Getting to Know* line does, however, apply very well to Grown-Ups.

To operate them properly, you have to get to know all your Grown-Ups' weird and wonderful ways. Learning how to handle them is about a thousand times more complicated than it is for regular appliances because Grown-Ups don't come with a list of product features and they don't come off an assembly line, so they're each unique! Also, while a toaster has a few buttons you can press, Grown-Ups have *hundreds*.

You might think you don't need to get to know your Grown-Up. If they've been knocking around since they changed your diapers you probably think you understand them and their funny little ways pretty well. But that's exactly where you are wrong!

I've just been interrupted. I'm writing this in the bedroom I share with Mandy. It's so tiny we call it the Cupboard. I'm curled up on the bottom bunk, which is the only private space I have in the world. Except it's not so private. Mandy just crashed in looking for her lip gloss.

"Have you stolen my lip gloss?" were her first words (unsurprisingly). She always accuses me of stealing things from her.

"No, I haven't stolen your stupid lip gloss. It's on the dresser."

She grabbed it.

"What are you doing? Writing about your interesting life?" she said in her best sarcastic voice, slamming out of the room.

I didn't bother replying. As if this were just some diary. Mandy has *no idea* about the importance of my work.

Anyway, to get back to Grown-Ups and their strange ways. You might already know them inside out, back to front and sideways . . . but there can be more to them than you think. And if you take the time to really study them, they can surprise you. It's a bit like wallpaper— if you stare at it long enough, you see more and more patterns.

★ ★ USEFUL HINT

Look beyond the random splodges of your Grown-Ups. See the patterns. Then you can be one step ahead of them.

I'm highly accomplished at analyzing the behavior of my mum. I know what every one of her hundreds of buttons does. You could say I've got a master's in mum studies. I certainly deserve one; I've put a lot of work in to make sure that I can predict her every move.

I know all Mum's little ways and routines. Like the fact that every Saturday morning she gets up before the rest of us, as she likes to putter about in the kitchen completely on her own, listening to her favorite music—stuff like Blur and the Lightning Seeds and Abba or anything by Tom Jones. If it's winter, she'll wear an old sweater of Dad's over her pajamas.

She uses the time to sort things out in her head. I've learned that she really needs this alone time and we *must not* interrupt her. If we leave her to her thoughts, she's in a much better mood for the rest of the day.

What else does she do? She enjoys ironing, which is strange. She adjusts the ironing board so she can iron sitting down while watching TV. This is always a good time to chat to her about anything that's bothering me, because she's relaxed. It's like she has all the time in the world—maybe because there's always loads of ironing!

She also does the ironing for our next-door neighbor Mr.

Cooper (or Creepy Mr. Cooper, as we call him, because he wears these awful slip-on shoes and lives alone). He pays her twenty pounds a week for doing his shirts and trousers. Mum puts the money in a bank account and calls it our rainy-day money. She's been doing his ironing for two years now, so she must have *over two thousand pounds* saved up! I wonder what we're going to do with it. . . .

You know what I'd like? For us to go somewhere hot, somewhere that's not Brindleton. White sand, blue skies, the gentle lapping of waves on the shore. Unfortunately, the fact that Mum's calling it rainy-day money makes me think she's got sensible things in mind for it, like mending our roof if it leaks or something equally tragic.

Mum's routines are always the same, so she's pretty predictable. She's a Pilates and aerobics instructor and a personal fitness trainer, so she can be found either in the community gym or power walking round the park with a client. If she's not in those places, she'll be at home doing the washing, ironing or cooking (though I try not to encourage this, as Mum's cooking is shockingly terrible. She has been known to burn a boiled egg). Once a month on a Saturday she'll take us shopping in Oxford, and every Friday night my Auntie Julie comes round to keep Mum company while I sleep over at Hannah's and Mandy goes out with her friends and Jack's asleep.

Knowing these routines makes operating Mum fairly straightforward.

You might not be so lucky; you might have a Grown-Up who's all over the place, being completely random. If so, try your best to gauge some sort of pattern—but you may just have to use your instincts and cunning to work out when it's best to approach or avoid them.

There are obvious times to approach a Grown-Up, like when they're in Happy Mode. But it is always advisable to do a little preparation ahead of your planned approach to ensure that they will be receptive to your demands.

★ USEFUL HINT

Preparation is essential. Do your research. DO NOT leave things to chance.

I take preparation extremely seriously. For example, a week before we're due to go to Oxford with my mum on our monthly shopping trip, I'll start to be more helpful around the house to make sure she's feeling all warm and grateful toward me when I ask her for new shoes. It works every time, unless we are particularly broke. So—in return for some light vacuuming—I get the shoes, or something else equally essential to my happiness.

I know this technique works with Mum because vacuuming is her most hated chore. However, this may or may not result in the same response from your Grown-Up—another reason to make sure you "get to know" them.

!WARNING

You may have prepared for weeks and judged the right moment to make your key operational maneuver, but BEWARE. Grown-Ups are—unfortunately—easily influenced by other Grown-Ups.

Gran Sutton (my dad's mum) thinks children should be seen and not heard, and probably wishes we were all still sent up chimneys or down into coal mines. There's **NO WAY** I'd ever try to operate Mum to my advantage while Gran Sutton was around. If I did, she'd make some unhelpful remark about how I should be grateful to even have a roof over my head and Mum would immediately agree with her.

My Auntie Julie, though, is the complete opposite and

definitely someone I encourage to visit. She always tells Mum to go easy on us

Auntie Julie's been completely obsessed with the band Take That for years, which is why I think she's never stopped acting like a teenager. It's Take That's fault she's *almost forty* and still living on her own, dreaming about meeting the perfect man.

How can anyone grow up when they've still got a poster of the singer Gary Barlow on their bedroom wall? At her age, how sad is *that*?

She goes on these dating websites and gets all excited about some wonderful man. Then, when she meets him, he never looks like his photo and nearly always ends up being crazy or perverted.

When Auntie Julie comes round on Fridays she forces Mum to drink at least one glass of wine. She then tells her about her latest adventures in the world of Internet dating. I think Mum enjoys hearing Auntie Julie's tales—they certainly make her laugh, anyway. I think they also make her glad she doesn't have to worry about the whole dating scene.

After Auntie Julie arrives and the wine is poured, but *before* I go off for my sleepover at Hannah's, is my Window of Opportunity. This is when Mum is off guard—it's the prime time for me to come clean about something I've done wrong, knowing that Auntie Julie will laugh it off and encourage Mum to do the same.

★★ USEFUL HINT

All Grown-Ups are much better behaved and far more reasonable in front of other people. They are far less likely to chase you with a meat cleaver when there are witnesses around. In times of crisis, bear this in mind.

Recently, I used the Window of Opportunity to tell Mum about breaking her third-favorite necklace. The conversation went as follows:

ME: Mum, you know how you can't find your necklace?

MUM: Yes, the one with the blue beads.

ME: Well, it's not lost. I broke it, but I was scared to tell you, so I threw it away.

(Scary, long pause.)

MUM: I can't believe it! How many times have I told you to be more responsible? I really liked that necklace.

ME: Sorry, Mum. It was an accident.

(Another scary, long pause.)

AUNTIE J: Remember when you drew all over our mum's best blouse in lipstick? She never did get the marks out, did she?

MUM: I was two at the time! Katie's thirteen, she should know better by now.

AUNTIE J: Well, at least she's come clean and said sorry, hasn't she? That's more than we did when we broke Dad's camera. We never owned up about that! You know, you've got to relax about things, Alison. Go on, have some more wine!

MUM (reluctantly): Well, I'm glad you apologized....

I suppose I'm lucky with Mum. I always know exactly where I am with her, which is very useful—from an operational viewpoint.

A fab pair of shoes in return for some vacuuming. Getting away with a major crime without a punishment . . . *just* the sort of results you too could achieve by simply getting to know your Grown-Up's routines, modes and functions. It's easy once you know how to press the right buttons.

Trust me, you're going to find this guide indispensable!

Saturday, August 1: 5:21 p.m.

ENVIRONMENT

Avoid positioning your Grown-Up where they may get wet, or too cold, or too hot. Extreme conditions will switch your Grown-Up into Grumpy Mode and will impair their function.

! IMPORTANT

DO NOT connect your Grown-Up to the electricity supply.

DO NOT place or drop any heavy objects on your Grown-Up.

DO NOT allow small children to operate your Grown-Up.

DO NOT dry laundry over your Grown-Up.

DO NOT write on or use paint on the surface of your Grown-Up.

DO NOT place your Grown-Up in the refrigerator.

NEVER operate your Grown-Up during a thunderstorm.

There are *lots* of other things you shouldn't do to your Grown-Up—like leaving them abandoned beside motorways or putting them in the post. I'm sure you're sensible enough to work this out for yourself. Basically, try not to trash them. They're no good to you if you break them, are they?

It's *very* important that your Grown-Up is comfortable in their environment. If they're not, they'll almost constantly be in Grumpy Mode.

⮕ GRUMPY MODE

Grumpy Mode is one of the easiest modes to identify because it's when everything in the world annoys your Grown-Up.

If your Grown-Up is in Grumpy Mode, then **DO NOT,** repeat **DO NOT** ask them for anything. Because even if you asked them if you could go to London to receive a bravery award from the prime minister for saving loads of people's lives, they'd probably say no.

The best course of action when your Grown-Up is in Grumpy Mode is to use the Avoidance Technique until they snap out of it. Listen carefully for where they are in the house (this is easy, as they are usually slamming doors, banging cutlery drawers and grumbling angrily) and make sure that you stay well clear of them.

Like all Grown-Ups, when Mum's in Grumpy Mode she's

totally unreasonable. I've learned the hard way to avoid her, or to use the more advanced technique of mode-switching.

Mum has been in Grumpy Mode for most of the day today—mainly because Jack brought Shame on the Family—which is very annoying, seeing as it's a Saturday. If Mum's in Happy Mode on a Saturday sometimes she'll take Rascal for his walk and let me do my own thing. If she's in Grumpy Mode, there's no chance and she'll purposely find millions of jobs for me to do.

It all began when a phone call interrupted Mum's peaceful puttering-about time. It was the library saying Mum needed to pay an enormous fine because Jack hadn't returned a whole pile of Doctor Who books.

When we got there, the librarian on duty was one of Mum's distant cousins, from the snooty branch of the family. You could tell by the way she was looking down her nose at us that she disapproved of:

a) the fine

b) the not-very-intellectual Doctor Who books

c) Jack's hair, which looks messy no matter how much Mum brushes it.

Over by the periodicals was a group of old ladies, including Gran Sutton. She was staring over at us with her beady eyes. Her and Mum have had a disagreement recently, so she's looking for any excuse to be harsh.

It was very quiet, as libraries tend to be. Then, totally out of the blue, Jack said, "Listen to this!" and did a huge, enormous, ear-shattering burp that lasted at least five seconds. This did *not* go down well.

The librarian said, "Really!" and there was a lot of shaking of heads and tutting noises from the old ladies by the periodicals, led of course by a very disapproving Gran Sutton.

That was it; Mum switched into full Grumpy Mode. I had to do *loads* of vacuuming when we got home and I had to walk Rascal. She's only just come out of it now.

! WARNING

Younger brothers and sisters can ruin your careful operational plans. They are completely unpredictable and can, in a matter of seconds, undo hours of careful preparation by switching your Grown-Up into an undesirable mode. When possible, use techniques such as distraction, threats or bribery to keep younger siblings under control.

What's great about my mum, though, is that she's not in Grumpy Mode too much, and her favorite environment is mostly hanging about the house with Jack and Mandy and me, which suits us just fine.

It's much easier to predict what your Grown-Up is about to do if they're right next to you on the sofa, watching TV. In Mum's case, I can predict she will do one of the following:

a) ask me to put the kettle on

b) at some point say "this is rubbish"

c) fall asleep.

Wednesday, August 5: 8:07 p.m.

 VIBRATION/NOISE

Most Grown-Ups dislike loud noise and vibrations. Be careful when using loudspeakers or amplifiers near your Grown-Up. Certain vibrations and magnetic fields can cause Grown-Ups to switch to Grumpy Mode. If this happens, act quickly. Grown-Ups can quickly progress into Irritated and even Angry Mode if the situation continues. And you don't want to go there, trust me.

Because of their highly stressful lives, most Grown-Ups want a bit of peace after a hard day. Which is why, for lots of them, loud music is a sore point.

For example, Hannah and me got in trouble with her mum, Auntie Susan, today. Apparently she could not hear herself think due to our playing music too loud when she was trying to sleep after a night shift at the hospital (she's a nurse).

I was lying on Hannah's bed doing exercises to try to build up my leg muscles and Hannah was on the floor painting her toenails a very attractive shade of scarlet. The next thing we knew, Auntie Susan came storming in with her face as red as Hannah's toenails, shouting at us to "turn that racket off" or she'd "throw the CD player out the window." Which we thought was a bit harsh.

"She's probably got PMS or menopause or something," said Hannah.

"No," I said, "she's just in Grumpy Mode."

"You're not going on about Grown-Ups and their modes and functions again, are you?" laughed Hannah, lifting her right foot up with remarkable flexibility and blowing on her toenails.

"I can't help being an expert," I said.

Mandy likes to play her music so loudly you can feel your teeth vibrating in your head. She's lucky Mum's not more like Auntie Susan, considering how incredibly annoying it is.

While Mandy's playing her loud music, she's usually in front of the mirror in the Cupboard. Mandy spends more time looking in the mirror than anybody I've *ever* met. I can't think why; I wouldn't want to be staring at that great big moaning face all day.

Actually, Mandy's quite pretty, if she would just smile now and again. Her best features are her blue eyes, which are exactly like Mum's. Her hair's thick and wavy and chestnut-brown. I'd love to have Mandy's hair instead of mine, which doesn't do anything except hang unattractively round my ears.

Mandy's not quite a Grown-Up, but she's always in Grumpy Mode about something—for example, if she gets a big spot on her chin or decides that she's massively fat (she's not), we all have to tiptoe around because at the slightest thing she'll switch into Angry Mode and say that we are trying to "ruin her life." I could do a whole guide on Mandy, she's becoming so complicated. . . . Maybe that could be my next project!

One noise Mum does hate is the sound of Mandy's mobile when she gets a text. It's this really annoying chiming noise and it goes off all the time because she's always texting her moronic friends things like "Wat r u wearing 2nite?"

Mandy and I used to be more like friends before she got obsessed with how she looks. I miss the old Mandy, the one who was more of a laugh. I remember one time we were on holiday, eating ice cream and Mandy shoved her cone up my nose, so I shoved mine up her nose. We were laughing so hard we were snorting vanilla chocolate chip.

It doesn't sound as funny now as it was at the time, but

that's the sort of thing I miss about Mandy. If I shoved an ice cream cone up her nose now it would ruin her makeup, which is the worst thing I could ever do. She'd go straight into Angry Mode. Maybe even Ax Murderer Mode. I'd have to leave the country and change my identity so she couldn't track me down.

Mandy's friends are all just like her. I got the idea to call them the Clones because they all dress and speak identically. They even wave their hands about in exactly the same way when they talk.

Mandy's main best friend (or should I say best Clone?) is called Lucy Parrish. Mandy won't let me talk to them when Lucy comes round, and won't even let me in the Cupboard when they are in there slapping on layer after layer of makeup with giant trowels.

It's incredibly unfair.

She's also constantly accusing me of stealing her stuff (like she did with the lip gloss the other day), even though she's always losing things. So it's "Katie, have you stolen my black eyeliner?" or "Katie, have you nicked my nail polish?"

Well, sometimes I do "borrow" her stuff—it's much better than mine. I just have to make sure Mandy doesn't catch me with any of it on.

★ Avoiding your older siblings can be just as beneficial to
your general well-being as avoiding your Grown-Up.

Talking about avoiding Grown-Ups—to get away from
Auntie Susan in Grumpy Mode, me and Hannah went out
to the park. Hannah wore her flip-flops to show off her toenails. Neil Parkhouse and Jonathan Elliott—who go to our
school—were there, but not Thomas Finch.

I think Neil Parkhouse likes Hannah, because he stole
one of her flip-flops and threw it over a fence. We made
him go and get it back. He was climbing back over when
he stepped in a great big pile of dog poo, which was *very*
hilarious.

"Did you know there are seven point four million dogs in
the UK?" commented Jonathan Elliott (who I reckon has a
giant book at home called *Little-Known Facts to Bore Your
Friends With*). "Between them they produce one thousand
tons of feces *every day!*"

It's typical of Jonathan to use a word like "feces."

"Well, I've got most of it on my shoe," muttered Neil.

Then Ben Clayden turned up!!! He was playing tennis

with Jake, one of my many cousins, but Hannah and I couldn't stare like we wanted to, as nobody must know how we feel.

On the way home, we came up with this brilliant plan to borrow a couple of tennis rackets so we can impress Ben. Neither of us has ever played tennis, but I'm sure we'll pick it up. It can't be *that* difficult, can it?

Thursday, August 6: 4:45 p.m.

OVERHEATING

Like all complex appliances, your Grown-Up can be prone to overheating. Unfortunately, this can happen very quickly. Overheating can be caused by a number of factors, but as every Grown-Up is unique, something that causes overheating in one Grown-Up may not cause it in another. The trick is to work out what their triggers are.

Overheating is easy to spot, because your Grown-Up's face will become extremely red. **BE VERY CAREFUL.** Overheating can lead to your Grown-Up's behaving irrationally and even dangerously. If overheating occurs, for your own safety *move away from the Grown-Up* until they have cooled down.

Today, when I got home from Hannah's, Mandy was cleaning out the garage! There's nothing more satisfying than seeing a brother or sister doing some hideous punishment while you watch from a safe distance, a smug expression on your face.

It turned out she had called Mum a loser, which caused

{31}

Mum to instantly overheat. Not only is Mandy cleaning out the garage, but she's also not allowed to go to Lucy Parrish's party tonight, which I know she thinks is the social event of the summer!

Mum will not put up with disrespect—that's one of her triggers. Now, if Mandy was an expert like I am, she would have known that. But she didn't. Which is why she is in trouble and I am lying on the sofa, relaxing. Life is *good*!

Mum's pretty normal as far as overheating is concerned. I mean, she doesn't get all stressed all the time like some Grown-Ups. She puts up with Mandy, who's constantly sulking, texting and generally being a drama queen. But she won't let Mandy go too far. Like today, for example. Sometimes overheating is good, I suppose; it shows people your limits.

With Mum, you usually know when you've crossed the line. Like last year when I wore her special scarf to the carnival in Oxford. It's dark green velvet, and she's always kept it draped over the back of the chair in front of her dressing table. I thought that as she never wore it, she wouldn't mind if I borrowed it.

I have *never* seen Mum instantly overheat the way she did when I came home that evening. Not only was I wearing her scarf, but (being incredibly classy) I'd managed to drip ketchup down it from a hot dog I'd eaten.

She ripped it off me and kept yelling that I had no right to borrow it without asking, blah, blah, blah, shout, shout, shout.

It turned out that it was a present she'd got from Dad way back when they were teenagers, but *how was I to know that?* You'd think it was some valuable priceless antique the way she carried on.

That was when I realized you have to be aware of your Grown-Up's triggers. Luckily, I'd already developed a handy four-step plan to deal with a Grown-Up overheating:

OVERHEATING—THE FOUR-STEP EMERGENCY PLAN:

1) Move away from your Grown-Up. Do not stand in immediate proximity to your Grown-Up, as this could put you in physical danger.

2) Use calming language such as "Never Mind" and "Let's Put This in Perspective" and "Worse Things Happen at Sea."

3) Offer to help, even if you know there's nothing you can do. For example "Would you like me

to clean that from the ceiling?" or "Can I get

you a glass of water?" or "Would you like to

breathe into this paper bag?".

4) Wait for them to cool down. This can take

some time.

The four-point plan worked on the scarf occasion—I highly recommend point 4, which always works if points 1 through 3 haven't. Luckily for us, Mum tends to cool down quite quickly once she's got things out of her system.

Thursday, August 6: 5:15 p.m.

There are some images so terrible, so **HORRIFIC,** that they sort of burn themselves into your mind. Do you know what I mean? Well, that's exactly what's just happened to me.

I just went into the kitchen to get myself a glass of milk and what did I see? Mum's obviously cooled off after overheating earlier. In fact, she's so chilled out she is—right now—*dancing around the kitchen* to her Abba *Gold* CD! She's doing that Grown-Up dance where they have their elbows at their sides and do the strutting thing, and wiggle their bums. **SO EMBARRASSING.** I quickly retreated before she saw me, in case she tried to get me to join in.

Major cringe-fest.

!WARNING

If your model of Grown-Up is ancient (like, over thirty), they may react to a song they like with the "Dancing" and "Singing Along" operations, which means that they have switched to one of the worst modes of all.

EMBARRASSING MODE

Grown-Ups will always embarrass you at exactly the
worst moment. FACT.

Whether you're at school or shopping or anywhere in
public, you can *guarantee* that at some point your Grown-
Up will go into Embarrassing Mode. And at that exact moment, at least ten people you know will be walking past.

Grown-Ups who are very old (like, over forty) have often
passed into the "I Don't Care What People Think, I'll Say
What I Like" stage, which means that you can have little
or no influence over their Vocal Output. Be prepared for an
ENORMOUS Embarrassment Factor, as they say things
like, "I remember when you made a puddle all over the floor
at your birthday party when you were two. You were so
cute!"

Embarrassing Mode is, sadly, a very common occurrence
where all Grown-Ups are concerned. Again, I have devised
an ingenious and simple four-step emergency plan you
can follow:

EMBARRASSING MODE—
THE FOUR-STEP EMERGENCY PLAN:

1) Move away from your Grown-Up.

2) Do not stand in immediate proximity to your Grown-Up.

3) Pretend you don't actually know them.

4) Say "I've never seen this person before in my life."

Just *by existing* your Grown-Up is probably a huge embarrassment. My mum certainly is. I'm lucky no one else saw her dancing just now, but her cringe-worthy behavior doesn't stop there. A few weeks ago I got my first bra. I don't really need it, to be honest . . . but everyone else has one, so I talked Mum into it.

She took me into Oxford and treated me to a hot chocolate in this posh café to make a proper occasion out of it. It came served in a tall glass with whipped cream and marshmallows on top.

That's a typical Mum thing to do. She's very good at giving each of us what she calls "special time." She should win a prize, since most Grown-Ups suck at that, from what I hear.

But then she completely **RUINED** it in the shop. Anyone from here to Timbuktu could hear her shouting to the assistant about me needing a **"JUNIOR BRA"**! She might as well have used a megaphone. *Major* public humiliation.

☹ SAD BUT TRUE FACT

The more embarrassing the topic, the louder your Grown-Up's Vocal Output becomes.

And our Grown-Ups wonder why we don't want to hang out with them!!

My dad used to always embarrass us at family parties—he was a great fan of dancing and singing along.

He'd get up and dance even if nobody else did, and to make it worse he'd get all the words wrong. We've got this old video of him waving his arms around and treating us all to his own out-of-tune version of "I Can't Get No Satisfaction" at Auntie Julie's thirtieth birthday party. Sometimes I watch it with Mum and we laugh a lot . . . and sometimes we'll have a little cry.

I'd better tell you about what happened with my dad. He died four years ago. There. I've said it. It was really, really terrible for a long time, but *we're all right now*. Honestly.

Dad said he didn't want us to go about with giant sad faces for the rest of our lives because of what happened to him. He said he wanted us to go out there and make the most of life and do things to "make a difference."

This is how I'm hoping to make a difference, by writing this User's Guide. I want to make life easier for everyone out there whose Grown-Ups are—let's face it—*totally* out of control.

There are so many books about how Grown-Ups can manage the behavior of children and teenagers—but there's **NOTHING** about how we can manage *them.*

It's official! I'm breaking entirely new ground!

Friday, August 7: 3:00 p.m.

I'm hiding in my bedroom, unable to face the world ever again. Ever. Really. How ironic that just yesterday I was writing, in a superior manner, about Embarrassing Mode. Compared to my display at the park today, Mum dancing to Abba in the kitchen was actually incredibly cool.

Okay, here's what happened. Hannah and me dug out our mums' antique tennis rackets and some balls and rushed down to the tennis courts this afternoon because the other day we heard Ben Clayden say to Jake, "See you again Friday." Sure enough, they were there and the court next to theirs was empty. *Ka-ching!*

We strolled over casually.

"Didn't know you played," said Jake, looking at us in a suspicious way.

"All the time!" I said brightly, bouncing the ball up and down professionally. Hannah stood expectantly on the other side of the net, clutching her racket with both hands.

I took a deep breath and threw the ball in the air, hoping

for the best as I took a great swing at it. It flew straight into the net.

"Fault!" shouted Hannah, skipping from foot to foot, her ponytail swinging from side to side. I wanted to slap her.

I bounced the second ball, then threw it in the air. *Thwack!* The ball flew into Ben and Jake's court, hitting their net.

"Double fault!" trilled Hannah cheerfully.

"I know, why don't *you* try serving," I said as Jake threw our ball back over.

Hannah threw the ball in the air and missed it entirely. I decided not to shout "Fault" as I am not as childish as Hannah can be. She tried again and this time her racket made contact with the ball, which actually got over the net. I was so surprised I forgot to hit it back.

We decided to serve underhand, which is easier, and to just have a "knockabout." We were congratulating ourselves on a great rally (where we had hit the ball back and forth *four times* without missing it), when we realized Jake and Ben were looking highly amused.

"So, have you two put your names down for Wimbledon yet?" Jake called across as he and Ben effortlessly hit the ball to and fro like professionals.

Obviously we had to carry on for slightly longer, as stopping would only have been admitting defeat. So we went on with our pathetic attempts at tennis for another twenty minutes, trying to act like we were just having a bit of fun and like we actually *enjoyed* constantly having to get the ball out of the net or off the courts on either side.

It was then that I did the incredibly stupid thing. On TV, I'd seen tennis players leaping the net when they'd won a big tournament and it looked easy enough. So when we decided to stop, I had this idea that I'd try it. I thought it might impress Ben.

As I ran toward her, I could see the disbelief and fear in Hannah's eyes. The net loomed up, and at the last moment I knew with terrible, awful certainty that I couldn't make it, but I couldn't stop. In slow motion, I flew into the air and cleared the net with my first leg, then caught my other foot and landed flat on my face.

"Are you okay?" Hannah and Jake and Ben Clayden were standing over me as I sat up. I put my hand to my chin. There was blood.

"I think it's only grazed," said Ben matter-of-factly. "I'd get home and clean it up. What were you trying to do?"

I didn't have the heart to answer him. I just about managed not to cry. Hannah got me to my feet and led me out of the park.

Hannah could have gone on and on at me, asking me what I was thinking and why did I do it. But she didn't. She just took me home and handed me over to Mum and then she said she'd come over later with some chocolate. That's why Hannah is the most solid-gold, diamond-studded best friend and cousin anyone could ever have.

And I'm an idiot who should live in a cave, away from other humans.

Mum went into Sympathy Mode as soon as she saw my mutant chin.

⮞ SYMPATHY MODE

This is a very rare mode. Grown-Ups usually prefer to belittle your pain by saying things like:

"I've seen much worse than that."

"Double pneumonia? I TOLD you to wear your school hoodie."

"It's not the end of the world."

"Snap out of it."

or my personal favorite: "I don't think you'll die."

You will know when your Grown-Up is in Sympathy Mode because you will have their full attention. When this happens, *milk it for all it's worth* because it may not last very long.

"My goodness, what's happened?" Mum cried, immediately getting the Mr. Bump ice pack out of the freezer. I told her that I'd been going for a difficult shot and tripped—making my accident sound heroic rather than self-inflicted.

"Poor old you!" she said, leading me upstairs to the bathroom, where she slapped antiseptic cream on the cut, which hurt loads.

"Mum, *don't* make me go to Hannah's tonight," I begged, when I saw myself in the bathroom mirror. "I can *never leave the house again!*"

"I tell you what," she said as she put the cream back into the bathroom cabinet, "why don't we have Hannah here for a change and you can ask Louise too. We'll have a girls' night to cheer you up. I'll get some pizza."

Now, *that* is Sympathy Mode at its best.

★ ★ USEFUL HINT
★ To achieve full Sympathy Mode in your Grown-Up,
make sure you appear as a completely innocent victim.

I never would have triggered Sympathy Mode if I'd told my mum the absolute truth about how I got my chin injury. If I'd told her about the net leaping I'd have got the "Well, it's your own fault" response, which is much less satisfactory.

I enjoyed basking in Mum's sympathy for a while, but when I went up to the Cupboard to tidy it for Hannah and Loops, I started having flashbacks. This obviously means I have post–traumatic stress disorder! I kept seeing the look on Ben Clayden's face after he saw my Leap of Shame—a look of disbelief, pity and . . . I'm sure of it . . . *disgust.*

I crept under my duvet and wished that I could fast-forward my life by ten or twenty years in the hope that by then everyone might have forgotten about it. Rascal leaped on the bed and burrowed under the duvet, giving my face one lick and then running away, spluttering and sneezing. He'd obviously tasted the antiseptic cream.

11:30 p.m.

I must have fallen asleep, because I was woken up much later, when Hannah and Loops burst into the Cupboard, their hands filled with everything chocolatey that I love.

"Get out from under there!" cried Loops. "We can't eat all this alone!"

I stuck my head out and saw Loops wince at the sight of my chin, which apart from the graze was turning a lovely shade of purplish-blue. *Thank goodness it's not term-time,* was all I could think.

Tactfully, neither Hannah nor Loops referred to my super-uncool hang-your-sorry-head-in-shame-you-loser-idiot-of-the-century behavior of earlier, but took the more sensible approach of stuffing chocolate down me and talking about everything else except tennis-related subjects.

"So, *design your future!*" said Hannah. This is one of our favorite games.

"Me first!" said Loops. "Okay. I'm working as a top camerawoman, traveling all over the world filming buff movie actors.

"Then one day Robert Pattinson says, 'Beauty like yours should not be behind the camera; can you act?' And I say, 'I honestly don't know.' But I'm a natural, and soon I'm starring in lots of mega films earning millions of pounds *and* I win an Oscar. I retire when I'm thirty, and then I have four children with Rob (two sets of twins to cut down on being pregnant) and we live on an island in the Caribbean . . . but with a private jet so we can go to New York and London and places."

Loops threw herself down on the bed at my feet, eyes closed as she entered her blissful R-Patz-related fantasy.

"Sounds just about bearable," said Hannah, "if you like vampires. What about you, Katie-Cat?"

"I will spend the rest of my life in a remote Himalayan village, with only a donkey as my friend."

"Not the bald, toothless nun thing again," said Hannah, who knows me so well.

"Do they have donkeys in the Himalayas?" asked Loops.

"Come on, Katie," said Hannah, "stop wallowing."

"Okay," I said, "in the next year I surprise everyone by getting long sexy legs. I work as a supermodel for a few years but only to earn enough money to start my International Dog and Dolphin Rescue Center, on the next island along from Loops and R-Patz."

Normally I would have gone on to suggest that Ben Clayden would turn up one day and decide he wanted to stay and run the center with me. Today I did not have the heart for it. Anyway, Loops is getting sick of hearing Hannah and me going on about Ben Clayden.

"Sounds fab," said Hannah, not enthusiastically enough, "but listen to mine.

"War is about to break out between various countries.

Global warming is getting bad. Then I discover a way to establish world peace *and* stop global warming!"

"And that is . . . ?" Loops said, asking the question nobody was meant to ask.

"Lots of . . . yard sales?" said Hannah lamely, obviously not having thought things through.

We all dissolved into chocolate-fueled, screeching laughter.

Friends have a way of making things better.

Saturday, August 8: 2:00 p.m.

PROBLEMS OR QUERIES IN CASE OF MALFUNCTION

Please remember that if you have any problems or queries relating to your Grown-Up, there's no customer care team waiting to help you. If your Grown-Up suffers a serious malfunction, there is no service warranty and there are no guarantees whatsoever, five-year or otherwise.

You are on your own.

Hannah and Loops left this morning, strolling off in an annoyingly carefree manner to enjoy looking un-freaklike and being able to walk the streets without being ridiculed. Thanks to the magic of chocolate and laughter, they made me feel loads better last night.

Thank goodness for friends.

But there's one problem Hannah and Loops, and chocolate and laughter—and even an entire customer service team—can't help me put right. I'm on my own with this one, and it's going to take all of my expertise to fix.

Mum is suffering a **MAJOR** malfunction. My mum—yes, *my mum!—HAS A BOYFRIEND!*

The reason I haven't mentioned this before is because I've been in serious denial. And it feels so very, very, very, *very* wrong to use the word "boyfriend" in any way to do with my mum.

I suppose I thought that if I pretended it wasn't happening, he might just go away.

She only met him about six weeks ago, and he's called Stuart. He's a PE teacher and lives in Oxford.

Mum's out right now, shopping for something to wear on her date to the movies with him tonight, instead of staying at home, watching TV with us, where she belongs. Even now she should be looking after Jack. But no, the sad loser with the freakish chin has to do it. Mum's taken full advantage of the fact that there is **NO WAY** I can leave this house looking like this!

The fact that I am sitting here alone has made me realize I can no longer deny Stuart's existence.

I suppose my main problem with Stuart is that he's turned up in our lives at all. Our family's doing fine as it is. Everything was in pieces after Dad died, but we got through it—just the four of us. Things like that make you pretty close. That's why we don't need anyone else—we work okay as we are.

We've all got our routines and know what's what. And thanks to my expert techniques, I'm operating Mum smoothly and efficiently—so everybody's happy.

It's like Nan says—"If it ain't broke, why fix it?" That's exactly how I think of our family. We're not broken and we *don't* need fixing.

But suddenly, out of the blue, we've got this random bloke in a "No Logo" save-the-environment ecofriendly T-shirt turning up at *our* house, strolling into *our* living room, sitting on *our* sofa . . . and saying to Mum, "Yes, I will have a cup of tea, thank you, Alison."

I have to admit, Stuart's not a creep or a monster. In fact, Loops thinks he's good-looking, as he's outdoorsy and manly-looking in a Bear Grylls sort of way, though she's obviously not noticed his enormous nose. I also have to admit that he's not bigheaded or boring, or totally demented like the ones Auntie Julie finds on the Internet.

But . . . it's just wrong. Mum seeing someone.

Ever since Stuart's arrived on the scene, I've been noticing some small changes in Mum's behavior. She's started making more of an effort with her appearance and looking at herself in the mirror more. And the other night she said that she thinks we all watch too much TV! She's *never* said that before. It's obviously him.

Stuart's one of those Grown-Ups who really want to save the environment, and I think he's trying to convert Mum. She's been talking about building a compost heap in the garden *and* she's started recycling. Me and Mandy used to tell her she should recycle but she never listened to us. Now that *he's* told her she should, she's all for it!

He's tried hard to be nice to us, but he doesn't understand that he's already done the most unforgivable, plain wrong thing that anyone could do. He's *going out with our mum.*

I don't think he really understands kids either, which is weird, seeing as he's a teacher. For some bizarre reason, the other day he presented me with a solar-powered headlamp! He got one for Mandy too; said it would make it safer for us walking home in the dark. As if we would walk around in public with headlamps on!!!! He honestly *does not have a clue.*

It was so lame of him to try to buy our affection like that. Does he really think we'd let him have our mum in exchange for a headlamp?

Yesterday, not long after I came in with my freaky chin,

the phone rang. It was Stuart calling to make arrangements for taking Mum out tonight.

After she put the phone down, she looked all lit up from inside. There I was with a dangerous and possibly life-threatening chin injury and she was looking the happiest I've seen her in ages!

I've got a bad feeling about this.

NO REFUNDS, NO EXCHANGES

Your Grown-Up is nonreturnable. The manufacturer accepts no liability for their many faults. As they are probably, by now, slightly worn around the edges and past their best, if not seriously damaged, don't even think of trying to get your money back. You cannot upgrade your Grown-Up. There are *no refunds* and *no exchanges*.

I mean, what sort of a product is *that*?

You know what's totally annoying? You don't get to choose the Grown-Ups in your life in the first place. I've done a lot of thinking about that part of the deal. You can't conveniently exchange your Grown-Up for a better model or get compensation if they malfunction. You are stuck with what you get.

Imagine if you went to buy a new car, which is an important thing, and you turned up at the showroom and the person in front of you had just been handed a fantastic sports car, with heated seats and a built-in TV and games console, and then they brought you out a worn-out old wreck with a dent in the side and chewing gum stuck to the seats.

That's what it's like being born. You don't know if you're getting the sports car or the rusty old heap of junk.

Dad wasn't a sports car, but he wasn't a wreck either. He was something in between. He had his Porsche moments, you could say. Like the time when he took us to London and we had tea at this very posh hotel called the Dorchester. He joked that he wanted us to see "how the other half live."

There were times when he'd say, "Get in the car, we're going to the seaside!" and we'd just go, knowing that meant ice cream and rides and everything. He was never one to do things halfheartedly, not our dad.

But to be honest, Dad wasn't perfect. Like when he forgot to pick us up from elementary school the times Mum asked him to do it. His forgetting us was upsetting, because we knew Mum would have reminded him that morning and said, "Be sure you don't forget, Mike."

We'd be standing there, the last ones. He'd come rushing round after the teachers phoned him and apologize to them and charm them with his jokes. But what annoyed me most was he'd never apologize to us, he'd just say, "Let's be off then, girls."

So everyone has his or her bad moments; even my dad did.

Whatever sort of Grown-Ups you have in your life right now, there's no point feeling sorry for yourself about it. Make the best of it. After all, worn-out old cars can get fixed up and win at motor rallies, dents and all. And flashy sports cars can break down, or crash.

I suppose what I am trying to say is Grown-Ups are complicated and nothing is ever as simple as it seems. When you think you've got them figured out, they will *always* surprise you.

Mum's certainly surprised us, by getting a boyfriend. And right now, instead of me being the one out shopping for a hot date while she's stuck at home with Jack, it's the other way round. It's an abomination against the natural order of things.

Not that I mind looking after Jack. It's not difficult. He's happy on the computer. In fact, you could leave him there indefinitely. Archaeologists in the future will dig him up, still hunched there with his little skeleton hand clamped to the mouse.

But going back to how complicated Grown-Ups can be,

my point is that just when you get used to a situation, it has to go and change. The way Mum's acting definitely doesn't fit in with any routine I've ever seen before. I have no idea what will happen next and I'm not sure I like it. . . .

I bet Mum's buying something inappropriately sexy.

At least I can still influence her for her own good when she gets home. If she's bought something too sexy, I know exactly how to make her think it's slutty. Then she'll hide it in a drawer and never wear it. Ha ha!

I have another plan too. If Mum carries on going out loads, I know exactly how I can make her feel massively guilty. I'll just tell her that Jack's said something to me like "I miss Mummy." That should do it.

Okay, panic over. This so isn't a problem I can't handle. I am still in control.

Saturday, August 8: 9:30 p.m.

⊚ HAPPY MODE ⊚

Scientific studies—conducted by lab types in white coats—show that Grown-Ups in Happy Mode are much more likely to be cooperative and positive. It is essential to your well-being that you keep your Grown-Up in this mode as much as possible.

The best way to switch your Grown-Up to Happy Mode is by being the perfect daughter or son or grandchild or whatever you are to them. This may not be achievable all of the time—but all models of Grown-Ups come with good sensory perception and can identify when you are *making an effort.*

Not only was I babysitting Jack most of today while Mum bought herself a new slinky dress for going to the movies in (I mean, what's the point—it's dark in there!), but now I'm stuck home babysitting him again while she's actually *at* the movies. Mandy—having missed Lucy Parrish's party on Thursday—is now at Lucy's house catching up on all the Clone gossip. Even though she saw her yesterday. Tragic.

Mum was definitely in Happy Mode when she went out

tonight, looking very sophisticated and un-Mum-like. Stuart was dressed up as well. While he looked okay last week when he turned up in jeans and a T-shirt, he obviously has a problem when he tries to look cool. He'd changed his "No Logo" T-shirt for a freaky brown shirt that looked like it had been hand-woven by goats in Guatemala and—wait for it—a *knitted tie*. Which was *yellow*. He was still wearing his jeans, but he'd swapped his sneakers for some horrible burgundy slip-on shoes. Similar to those worn by Creepy Mr. Cooper. **OMG!!!!!!** Fashion-crime-scene alert. It was as if he'd raided some old man's wardrobe while blindfolded.

When he saw Mum come down the stairs, he practically went into Delirious Mode (the natural next step up from Happy Mode). He whistled and said, "You look stunning!"

Mum blushed and said, "So do you!"

!REMINDER TO SELF:

Suggest to Mum she get an eye test.

Mandy was still there at that point, and we both retreated into the front room. "Please pass me a bucket so I can puke my guts up," hissed Mandy, under her breath.

"Sorry, need it myself," I replied.

It was odd to see Mum in Happy Mode without it being due to me, Jack or Mandy, or even Auntie Julie. It's usually us who make her laugh or cheer her up. Tonight she seemed a different kind of happy too. . . .

Mum used to be in Happy Mode all the time back when Dad was alive, but it's harder and harder to remember that. For a long time after he died, she wasn't. That's why switching her into Happy Mode as much as possible has become one of my main responsibilities when operating her.

For example, recently Mum's been worrying about the tiny, almost invisible wrinkles round her eyes and on her forehead. "I'm getting old," she says in Sad Mode. So I say, "No you're not, you're beautiful," which puts her straight back into Happy Mode.

Not that it's that easy to succeed every time. The other day I caught her standing in her bra and panties studying herself in the full-length mirror on the back of the bathroom door.

"Look at my saggy boobs and stretch marks," she said. "I'm a state."

I didn't know what she meant. Mum is super-fit due to her sporty job. But when I looked closely I could see what she was on about. Her boobs *did* look slightly (but only a little) on the droopy side, and I could see a few faint silvery red stretch marks on her thighs and stomach.

"You look great," I said. "I mean, no one would ever know you've had *three children*."

"It's just, I never thought I'd have to worry like this at my age," she said, sounding down. "I never had to think about these things when I was with your dad."

I don't know why she thinks she has to worry about these things now, but I felt sorry for her, looking so unsure of herself. Just as I was thinking what else to say, Mandy came breezing out of the Cupboard.

"Mum, you're a complete stunner," she said.

I have to admit that even though we've always done our best and tried to keep Mum cheerful, she's been more in Happy Mode since Stuart has been around. Which I suppose is good. I mean, Mandy came in *an hour late* on Wednesday and Mum didn't even notice, when she'd normally be having a fit.

I don't know if I like the fact that Stuart's taking over some of my role as expert mode-switcher. But then again, maybe I shouldn't worry. Mum's in Happy Mode, so it's one less thing for me to do. Why is life never simple?

10:35 p.m.

I've been thinking more about what I've just written

while in the bathroom experimenting with covering my chin with foundation and concealer. I'm not doing a very good job. Mum said that if I can't manage it myself she'll help me tomorrow so that I can go out in public.

She's brilliant with makeup. When we were little, she used to do face-painting at parties and she was great at it. She still makes Jack into a tiger now and again, though he's beginning to think it's not cool, which is a shame.

You've got to love Jack. He can put any of us in Happy Mode just by being his weird self. He's great at lifting anyone's mood—even if it's normally by being disgusting. Like tonight when I went into his room to put out his light.

He said, "If someone said that you had to eat a whole room full of other people's boogers or be shot, what would you do?"

"I'd rather be shot," I said.

Jack nodded in agreement. "Me too. But—be honest—would you eat *one* booger or be shot?"

"I'd have to eat the booger," I admitted.

"Eeeeeeeeeoouuuu*yuck*!" Jack rolled about on his bed in delighted disgust. "Booger eater! Booger eater!"

Despite all my worries about Mum and Stuart, I had to smile.

Sunday, August 9: 10:27 a.m.

!WARNING

DO NOT operate your Grown-Up for more than sixteen consecutive hours. Your Grown-Up is not designed for continuous operation. After sixteen consecutive hours, most models of Grown-Up will automatically switch to Sleep Mode.

➦ SLEEP MODE

Sleep Mode in Grown-Ups is an easy one to spot. Eyes shut. Mouth open. Loud, eardrum-shattering snoring. This is usually brought on by Tired Mode, which can be either because of your continuous operation or by them working or partying too hard.

Be aware it may just be because your model of Grown-Up is ancient and exhausted.

Mum was out so late with Yellow Tie Man (as I'm now calling him) last night, I *didn't even hear her come in!* And I was up until 1:13 a.m.! Well, that was the last time I looked at my alarm clock before going to sleep myself.

I brought her a cup of tea quite early (for me) this morning to get some answers. She just grunted at me and pulled the duvet over her head. She hadn't even taken her makeup off the night before! I could see mascara on her pillow. Gross.

I went back with another cup an hour later and she hadn't touched the first one. She told me to go away and let her sleep in peace.

"What about Jack?" I said. "You're his mother, you've got to feed him!"

"He's old enough to get his own breakfast, and if he can't, you can help him," she mumbled. "Now go away and let me sleep."

"When did you get in?" I asked innocently. But she didn't answer.

TROUBLESHOOTING TIP

"My Grown-Up Will Not Start"

There could be several reasons for this:

1) Your Grown-Up had a late night the night before.

2) Your Grown-Up is in Sad Mode.

3) Your Grown-Up is seriously ill. Call 999 immediately and possibly save their life.

Mum usually only needs about seven hours' sleep. So that means she was out until at least three a.m.—or perhaps even later. *Maybe she was out all night!*

12:30 p.m.

This is getting serious. It's lunchtime and Mum's *still* in Sleep Mode. Even Rascal trying to lick her face won't rouse her. She just rolled over!

Mandy has come back from Lucy's house and she agrees with me that Mum has been up to no good. We are Officially Disgusted.

I tried to get her to get up for lunch but she just groaned. Then I reminded her that she's supposed to help me to cover up my chin before I go out later.

"You can do it yourself, love," she said. "I've got to catch up on my sleep. You don't mind, do you?"

And before I could say, "Yes I *do* mind, actually," she was snoring away again. Which means that I've got to do my chin all by myself when she specifically said she'd help if I needed her—which I do. How rubbish is that?

This is an example of Grown-Up Deviant Behavior. I am trying to think of anything I could have done differently to prevent this situation. After all, I'm supposed to be writing a guide about smoothly operating your Grown-Up, so this is quite embarrassing.

But what could I do? How do you stop your Grown-Up from going off the rails when you least expect it? I will have to give this a lot of thought.

2:19 p.m.

I've finally cracked it! No, not Mum (sadly)—my chin. I can now go out in public again! Two parts beige foundation, one part Mum's expensive concealer she uses for the shadows under her eyes. She never noticed me get it from her dressing table because she was so deeply asleep. Ha ha!

Hannah is coming round any minute and we're going to the park. The reason we're going is this—Neil Parkhouse casually asked Hannah if she was going there and she said she was, showing no loyalty to Ben Clayden whatsoever.

8:23 p.m.

Well, I wish I hadn't gone. Neil Parkhouse, Jonathan Elliott and Thomas Finch were all there. Thomas, of course, would not look at me due to the dumping business. He looked great; he seems to have grown taller and he's got a fantastic tan from Spain.

Thomas was standing beside Loops, while Neil hung around Hannah and I was left with Jonathan Elliott.

As well as knowing lots of little-known facts, Jonathan's one of those brainiac types who are in the top set of everything at school and who win prizes for science projects. He's a year older than the rest of us and a lot of girls think he's good-looking. I sort of agree, if you ignore his slightly sticking-out ears. Anyway, according to all the magazines Mum reads, it's not supposed to be about looks, you're supposed to look at people's "inner beauty."

The problem is, when I try to look at Jonathan Elliott's inner beauty I just see a bighead-nerdy-know-it-all. How disappointing is *that*?

I braced myself for one of his rambling lectures about splitting the atom. But he didn't even start. He just turned to me and looked searchingly into my eyes.

"So," he said, "why exactly is your chin brown?"

When I got back from the park, Mum had finally surfaced. It's so unlike her to sleep most of the day! This has left me completely confused. I thought I was an expert in Mum's start-up patterns. After all, I've studied them carefully.

➤ START-UP OPTIONS

There is no "Quick Start" with Grown-Ups. Generally they are very slow to get going, especially in the mornings. Many cannot perform even the simplest operation or function without the essential fuel known as a "Cup of Coffee."

However, there are some exceptions to this rule. Some Grown-Ups wake early, such as the over-the-age-of-seventy-five models. Many of these models have got up, had their breakfast, washed up and done the crossword before seven a.m. Which gives them nine hours to fill before Countdown.

My Great-Grandma Peters is eighty-seven, so she's definitely an exception to the slow-start rule. She gets up before six and by the time it's ten o'clock she's done everything she needs to do. From then on it's just filling the hours. She can't exactly go for a cross-country run or join the gym, so it's daytime TV and nosing out of her window, plus endless cups of tea with anyone who cares to pop in.

Great-Grandma Peters watches so much TV she thinks she actually knows all the celebrities personally.

If I go to her house, no matter what the time of day,

there's usually someone else there who's had the same idea. Sometimes there are too many people for her tiny living room and she has to say, "Go on, clear off, the lot of you!"

What's funny is that even though she's always got people at her house, Great-Grandma Peters is convinced that she's lonely and neglected.

That's Grown-Ups for you. No matter how old they are, they never seem to learn. Which leads me on to a little bit of general advice.

A NOTE ON THE OLDER MODELS OF GROWN-UP

Grown-Ups aged over thirty must be treated with extra caution, due to the number of years they have been operating. They can be suffering from a "Midlife Crisis"—an age-related condition that causes erratic mode swings but usually passes with time.

⇨ MIDLIFE CRISIS MODE

If your Grown-Up starts asking you whether what they are wearing makes them look old, or they are dressing totally inappropriately for their advanced years (losing what little dignity they once had), they are in Midlife

Crisis Mode. They may organize school reunions and go on and on about the good old days.

Be warned: It is tragic to witness and may result in Embarrassing Mode, which will usually be at its worst when your friends come round.

Mum must be in Midlife Crisis Mode—that's the only explanation I can think of for her acting so strangely and wanting to go out with Yellow Tie Man, who rolled off the production line five years after her. He's a younger man, so in her desperate midlife crisis she's obviously latching on to him to try to recapture her lost youth! *That's* why she's worrying about the wrinkles and trying to act younger than she is by staying out all night.

While I think Mum is pretty old (I mean, she's *over thirty*), she's actually young compared to lots of my friends' Grown-Ups.

Mum was eighteen when she had Mandy. That's only three years older than Mandy is now. **YIKES!** She and my dad were at school together and started going out when they were seniors. Dad was supposed to either study heating engineering or train as a chef after graduation, but when Mum got pregnant they got married and he got the first job he could: driving a van for the parcel delivery firm where Granddad Williams (Mum's dad) worked.

Dad said it was the best thing that could have happened and he loved his job, but I think he just said that so Mandy wouldn't feel bad about being born.

Thursday, August 13: 4:39 p.m.

Six *whole days* after my serious and traumatic chin injury, and Mum hasn't even asked how I am feeling about it! She doesn't even care about making me go out in public—she sent me (and my chin) to the minimart to get some milk yesterday. I begged her to let me stay hiding at home, but she wasn't having any of it.

Of course, when I got there, Nan shouted from the other end of the shop, "Look at you, Katie Sutton! With that bruising on the end of your chin, you look as if you've got a *goatee*! You look like a *man*!"

I looked around, expecting to see Ben Clayden. But there was no sign of him. Then I saw Thomas Finch staring at me from behind the bargain DVDs. I had to hide my chin behind a two-liter carton of milk. Not sure if I got away with it.

Mum doesn't seem to care about my humiliations. She's too busy looking disgustingly dreamy. This must be down to her needing to be in Sleep Mode. I refuse to be disheartened by Mum's recent selfish behavior. It's just a phase, due to her meaningless fling with Yellow Tie Man. It's just Midlife Crisis Mode. It's not like they're in love or anything.

PERFORMANCE OPTIMIZATION

To achieve optimum performance from your Grown-Up, it is important to acquaint yourself with their Operating Modes. Familiarization with their complex modes is essential in order to operate your Grown-Up with maximum efficiency.

That's the trouble with Grown-Ups having power over our entire miserable lives. It all comes down to the mode they are in.

When I really needed Mum to help me save my social life by covering up my mutant chin, she completely let me down by being in Sleep Mode. And there was nothing I could do. I have to remember that it's not my expertise in question, it was just a problem with the timing.

★ USEFUL HINT

Timing is everything. Choose your moments carefully and be alert to unexpected chances. Also, remember that you can make opportunities. Be creative!

When I bought my fabulous pair of shoes and miniskirt for the school dance back in April, I got home from my shopping trip and saw that Mum was in Grumpy Mode. She'd filled in for a friend teaching a step aerobics class and one of the people in the class had fallen off their step and made a complaint to the leisure center manager about Mum making the routine too difficult.

"That's the last time I do anyone a favor!" she was moaning.

So there was *no way* I'd have shown her my stuff at that moment. Otherwise she'd have told me the shoes were too high and the skirt was too short and I should take them back to the shop immediately. I couldn't risk this, as both Hannah and Loops had, that very day, bought almost identical shoes and miniskirts. If I didn't have them too, I would be an Outcast.

So what I did was this: I was incredibly helpful round the house. I did some light vacuuming (remember my top tip from earlier?), and then guess what, Mum's not in Grumpy Mode anymore. She's telling me that I'm a great help to her and a good girl. (Really, I'm not. I'm a calculating fraud.)

That evening, I waited till Mum was halfway through the ironing and her favorite soap, as I knew she'd be totally relaxed then. When I walked into the living room wearing the outfit, she choked slightly on her cup of tea, but—thanks to my careful groundwork of being the perfect daughter for the afternoon—she didn't tell me to take them back. In fact, she started rambling on about her first miniskirt and what she used to do when she was a teenager. (She was in Been There, Done That Mode, a particularly irritating mode.) Too much information, to be honest . . . but total parental approval.

Now, *that's* what I call Performance Optimization at its best.

7:48 p.m.

I'm very bored, so I text Hannah. I've got to check up on her and Loops, otherwise they could get into all sorts of trouble.

ME: how u doing?

HANNAH: at park w Loops Neil+T+J hows ur chin?

ME: purple

HANNAH: LOL

ME: nan sed it looks like beard

HANNAH: Thomas F says she sed goatee

(At this point I just about died of embarrassment, but I had to think of something else to say so I didn't appear too bothered.)

ME: r u going to shops for choc?
HANNAH: U go Urself?
ME: Not w beard
HANNAH: Loops says hi
ME: me too hv fun kisses!
HANNAH: !!!!! C U L8R

Great. So to Thomas Finch I am now Goatee Girl. Fantastic. I see my future clearly now: as a *bearded,* bald, toothless, donkey-riding nun.

Saturday, August 15: 3:20 p.m.

 SMITTEN MODE

Smitten Mode is when Grown-Ups get all infatuated with someone and lose what little dignity they once had (if they ever had any, which is unlikely). This mode is one step further than Fancying the Pants Off Mode but not as serious as Love Mode. If your Grown-Up can't stop talking about somebody, or if they keep staring into space with an idiotic look on their face and sighing contentedly, they are probably in Smitten Mode.

Be aware this may cause them to become absentminded, which is not ideal if they forget important things, like your allowance.

You know how I said at the beginning of this guide that I know a thing or two about Grown-Ups? Like I can give great advice? Maybe I spoke too soon.

Today something happened that made me *question my abilities*. I was so sure Mum was just having a midlife crisis. I never considered she might actually be in Smitten Mode. I thought I could predict her behavior. But no matter how predictable you think they are, Grown-Ups can still shock you.

❗WARNING

Grown-Ups can take you by surprise. Be prepared for anything. At all times.

Mum's shocking behavior is all Yellow Tie Man's fault. Today he went into Reckless Mode, probably influenced by being in Smitten Mode.

➥ RECKLESS MODE

If Grown-Ups act the opposite of how they expect you to act, without any apology or awareness of their massive double standards, they are in Reckless Mode. This is a highly dangerous mode that hampers smooth operation.

This morning Stuart turned up out of the blue on our doorstep with a bunch of about thirty red roses.

This set my alarm bells clanging madly straightaway. I mean, I thought this was just a fling. But if you know the language of flowers you'll know that red roses mean "I love you." Which is **NOT** good.

He stood there smiling hopefully, peering through the armful of blooms. At least he had ditched the tie and was back in his usual T-shirt and jeans.

Even Mum was embarrassed by his ridiculous display.

"Did you walk all the way from the bus stop with those?" she asked.

We knew what she was worried about. She was thinking about her entire family—especially the disapproving and beady eye of Gran Sutton—and everyone else in the village twitching their curtains and having a great laugh at Yellow Tie Man walking along like a prize idiot with his mobile rose garden.

"Yes!" said Stuart proudly, and we could see that all sense had left him. If he'd been a dog, he'd have had his ears back and his tail would have been wagging madly.

I almost felt sorry for him, until I remembered how much Mum's behavior has changed in the last two weeks thanks to him. She's so different! Suddenly she's got her own plans, instead of fitting in with mine. It was a relief to see that she did not seem to be in Reckless Mode as well. (Or so I thought . . .)

"You'd better come in," said Mum in an abrupt voice. You could see the disappointment on Stuart's face. *At least he must have got the message now,* I thought happily. Nobody could ever in a hundred million *squillion* years replace our dad, not *ever*. No matter how many red roses they turn up with.

I looked across at Mandy, who was making herself some toast, and she smirked at me, equally triumphant. I realized that I had somebody on my side and we were obviously thinking exactly the same thing: *zero points to Stuart*. Jack bounced into the kitchen just at that moment and stared at the roses, puzzled.

"Are we going to a funeral?" he asked. Typical of Jack to say the right thing at the right moment—I could have hugged him. Stuart looked even more miserable and uncomfortable.

But in the time it took to boil the kettle, Mum had softened.

"They're *beautiful*, Stuart," she relented, arranging them in the big blue vase from the display cabinet. "They're really, really lovely."

I think she felt bad about being short with him and was trying to make up for it.

Stuart looked like he'd won the lottery, the Euro Millions rollover.

"I've never bought anyone flowers before," he said, his face all flushed with pleasure. "I don't know why I did it. I haven't even checked if they're—"

But before he could finish going on about organic produce or sustainable sources or whatever he'd been going to say, Mum was *kissing him*. Right in front of her children, right there in the kitchen!

!WARNING

When one Grown-Up goes into Reckless Mode, it can cause others to do the same. It's infectious. Like a terrible, unstoppable disease.

I stood there thinking, *Who is this woman, and what has she done with our mum?*

I don't understand how this is all happening, why she's even interested in him. I mean, *how could she be?* He has an enormous nose and he owns a *yellow knitted tie*!

It would be fair to say that we were all seriously traumatized by what we witnessed. No child should have to see such a sight without getting counseling.

Mandy turned round, pretending to be looking for something in the kitchen drawer. Jack, inexplicably, put his fingers in his ears. And me? I stood with my mouth wide open like a human flycatcher.

☹ SAD BUT TRUE FACT

It's a horrible fact of life, but Grown-Ups snog too. They take something that is perfectly acceptable in young and attractive people and turn it into a disturbing and tragic act.

★ USEFUL HINT

The only solution when you witness Grown-Ups kissing is to leave the vicinity of the incident immediately or scream loudly. It is essential that you protect yourself from major trauma, as this could lead to you needing years of therapy. If you find it hard to obliterate the image of the kissing incident from your mind, try to replace it with another more pleasant image—like trench warfare.

I wished that I had a magic remote control in my hand, with a guaranteed way of stopping the shocking scene. Even hitting Pause while I thought up some brilliant scheme would have helped. Better still, Rewind. If I could have rewound Stuart all the way out of the door backwards and down the street and back to the flower shop, I would have done it. But I was powerless.

The kiss probably only lasted a few seconds, but it felt like it was going on forever. I thought the horror would never end.

Mandy sidled up to me and hissed, "The Cupboard, *five minutes*."

I was there (two minutes early), and somehow Mandy had got Jack rounded up as well. Soon the three of us were all sitting on my bed (the lower bunk of course, the curse of the younger child) having our first Council of War.

"Was it just me," said Mandy, "or was that one of the *grossest* things you have ever seen in your entire life?"

"It was more yuck than if Mum was kissing one of the Ood," said Jack. The Ood are aliens in *Doctor Who*. The ones with giant tentacles coming out of their faces.

"No," I said, "it was **WORSE** than that. I will *never* get it out of my head."

Just thinking about it made me realize that Mum wasn't just in Reckless Mode—she was in Smitten Mode too.

"Look," said Mandy, "I thought he was an idiot, but he's not, is he? Not if he can get Mum to *kiss* him in the kitchen in front of her own kids. She's obviously massively into him! If it carries on like this, Mum and Stuart might get married and he might try to be our new dad!"

"No way!" said Jack.

"*Yes* way," said Mandy. "And who wants that to happen?"

I shook my head. I can't imagine having Yellow Tie Man here all the time . . . it would feel weird.

Jack looked thoughtful.

"Maybe he could stay if he took us to Disney . . . ," he said.

Jack has this idea that when your mum gets a new boyfriend they automatically take you to Disney World or Disneyland, since that happened to two different friends of his at school. So now that Stuart's on the scene, Jack's obviously waiting for the invitation.

Mandy rolled her eyes.

"Jack, that is *so* not the *point*! Listen, if we all work together we can probably get rid of him before school starts. Are you with me?"

"Definitely!" I said. Jack was still staring into space. No doubt thinking about meeting Mickey Mouse. Really, he has no idea.

8:23 p.m.

I phoned Hannah an hour ago. She was, quite rightly, disgusted on my behalf.

"So they were practically *having sex* in your kitchen!" she shouted. "That's like child abuse!"

Which was just like Hannah, making a drama out of anything. You get like that when you live in Brindleton, where nothing ever happens.

"Shhhh! No, not quite. But it was as bad as if they were," I hissed. "Mandy and Jack and me have decided he's *got to go.*"

"I'll help if you want," offered Hannah, "I've got a brilliant idea! Let's pretend he's got terrible body odor whenever we see him. I could actually *faint* if you want."

"Hannah, that's just immature," I said. "We've got to be *much* cleverer than that. Especially now that Mum is in Smitten Mode! Listen, I'll let you know when I have a proper plan. You phone Loops and fill her in and we'll talk about it tomorrow."

So that's where we are now. I'm at home babysitting, again. Tonight Mum is out being wined and dined by Yellow Tie Man in some posh restaurant that teachers who wear yellow ties go to. They're probably drinking champagne and telling each other how wonderful they are.

One good thing is that my chin seems to be improving, so I no longer look bearded. And tomorrow I'll see Hannah and Loops for some moral support. Maybe when I go to sleep I'll dream up a master plan to switch Mum out of Smitten Mode immediately.

I'll need every single one of my skills in understanding and controlling Grown-Ups to pull this one off.

Sunday, August 16: 10:00 a.m.

MODE-SWITCHING

It is important that you become skilled in switching your Grown-Up from mode to mode, in order to ensure that you stay in control. If your Grown-Up is stuck in one mode, such as Smitten Mode, for example, this can seriously impair essential everyday functions. If this occurs, try to force them to switch to another mode, such as Angry Mode or Terrified Mode.

I need to get better at following my own advice. When Mum and Stuart were kissing disgustingly yesterday, I should have leaped up and shouted "Fire!" or "Look—a werewolf!" But I was too shocked.

Mum—yet again—did not come home while I was still awake. Last night, after I spoke to Hannah, it was the Saturday night of any teenager's dreams . . . (yes, I'm being sarcastic and bitter) . . . Rascal, Jack and me played Monopoly. Well, Rascal didn't play Monopoly, obviously.

Jack won, and I *didn't even let him.*

It's official. My eight-year-old brother is brainier than I am.

If I was less of a dimwit perhaps I could work out how to use mode-switching to better effect than I'm managing.

I must remember to play the guilt card with Mum to stop her from going out so much. I'll do that later.

I don't want to spoil things for Mum, but I also don't want her rushing into things and doing things she might regret. She's my Grown-Up and my responsibility. I am only thinking of her welfare, like any careful owner . . . I mean, daughter.

2:00 p.m.

Went up to the park earlier and saw Hannah and Loops, who were dying to hear the lowdown on Mum and Yellow Tie Man.

Loops looked so *weird*! She'd straightened her hair, which made her head look half its normal size. I'm used to her hair being all crazy and fab and curly, and the straight look didn't suit her at all.

But as she seemed so very pleased with it, Hannah and I didn't want to spoil her good mood. So we lied. We said we liked it.

I wore my blue T-shirt because it was hot (the weather, not the T-shirt) and my denim shorts with the patches on them. I'd done a much better job of concealing the remaining bruising on my chin, so I was feeling better about being in public. We sat on the row of three swings. Swings are a great place for holding a conversation, if you ignore the sad faces of the kids who can't go on them and their Grown-Ups in Annoyed Mode.

"I heard about him walking around with about a hundred *roses*," said Hannah. "Nan saw him and she rang my mum straightaway. She said, 'A fool and his money are soon parted.'"

"He seems nice, though," said Loops, who kept moving her head around to flick her straight hair. Hannah and I stared at her.

"Are you *joking*?" I said. "Don't you *see* what he's trying to do?"

"Make your mum happy?" suggested Loops. She can be so dense sometimes.

"He's trying to change *everything*," I carried on, and I could feel my heart thumping incredibly fast. "Mum's so distracted she forgot Jack's dentist appointment last week! If all of Jack's teeth rot and fall out, it's Stuart's stupid fault!"

I saw Neil Parkhouse and Thomas Finch strolling across the soccer field toward us, but I didn't care.

I was surprised at how worked up I was about Stuart and Mum. I didn't know how strongly I felt till it all came rushing out.

Loops crossed her arms. She can be very stubborn.

"Well, maybe you should give him more of a chance," she said. "At least they're happy. My mum and dad are either ignoring each other or fighting about who puts the rubbish out."

I jumped off the swing and turned on her. "Why do you always have to take the other person's side and argue about it? Why can't you just be a friend? By the way, I *hate* your hair like that!"

I stomped off, bumping straight into Thomas Finch. My face was red with anger. I probably looked like a demented tomato.

"Whoa!" he said, holding his hands up. "I surrender!"

He was actually *talking* to me (!) and he gave me this fantastic smile . . . but it was totally spoiled, seeing as I was still so mad at Loops. I pushed right past him and marched all the way home, seething.

As I got in the door, the phone was ringing. It was Hannah on her mobile.

"Loops is sorry she wasn't more supportive," she said,

in her careful, peacemaking voice, "but she's really upset about what you said about her hair. Katie, she's crying and *everything*!"

I could hear a sort of high inhuman wailing in the background. It was either Loops or Hannah's cat being tortured. I assumed it was Loops.

So I had to meet them at Hannah's and tell Loops that her hair was really cool . . . and *then* she said that I was right and it *did* look weird . . . and *then* we told her we preferred it curly but whatever it looked like she was incredibly attractive and beautiful . . . and *then* we ate a lot of chocolate cookies and said sorry to each other hundreds of times.

Friends are hard work sometimes.

5:24 p.m.

Now I am back home, with the house to myself, chilling out. For some reason I keep thinking about Thomas Finch saying "I surrender!" and giving me that smile of his. I was in too much of a mood to appreciate it. Typical. And there he was, surrendering. . . . What am I *thinking*? It must be the hot weather making me confused.

Still can't think of a way to switch Mum and Stuart out of this hideous Smitten Mode. I need them to realize that even though they fancy each other, they don't have *anything* to say to each other.

Mum pretends to be interested in all Stuart's talk about the environment, but she must be bored out of her mind. When she stops being smitten she'll stop hiding her boredom. She'll be yawning her head off right in front of him, and he'll be wondering why he's with a woman who's never been camping in her life!

You might be wondering how my mum met Stuart, a PE teacher from Oxford (which is almost ten miles from Brindleton). A man *almost five years younger than her*.

Brindleton is in an "Area of Outstanding Natural Beauty," according to a sign by the village hall. I wouldn't agree, but then again I've lived here all my life, so it looks pretty ordinary to me. There are footpaths for people to walk along, and sometimes you see them with their backpacks and their socks over their trousers. Striding along Enjoying Nature. Singing "Val-de-ri! Val-de-ra!"

That was Stuart just a couple of months ago—only I don't think he was doing the socks thing or singing. Though you never know.

One of our local farmers thinks it's a great joke to keep bulls in a field that has a public footpath going through it.

He hates townies. Stuart got to that particular field and found himself staring down about twenty-five young bulls, a few of which started toward him. He ran for the nearest fence, which was made of barbed wire but had a tree branch hanging over it. He climbed on the branch, but it snapped and he found himself sitting on the fence with his trousers ripped and bits of sharp barbed wire sticking into his bum.

Whenever I remember Stuart and Mum kissing in the kitchen, I shut my eyes and imagine him on that barbed-wire fence. It makes me feel much better.

★ USEFUL HINT

Use advanced visualization techniques when Grown-Ups annoy you. There are many scenarios you can imagine the Grown-Up in:

a) on the toilet with very bad constipation

b) standing in front of a firing squad

c) being chased by badgers.

Let your imagination run wild.

Stuart pulled himself off the fence (imagine your own sound effects) and limped to the nearest road. He decided to knock on the door of the first house he came to and ask for help.

Mum was at home, cooking tuna pasta surprise. The surprise was the pickled gherkins. Mum, as I mentioned earlier, is a hideous cook.

When he appeared and explained what had happened, she got the medical kit out and showed him to the bathroom. Then—this is the *worst* part—she gave him a pair of Dad's old trousers from a bag she'd never got round to taking to the charity shop.

When I got home, Stuart was sitting at the kitchen table having a cup of tea, but as soon as he saw me he ran off as fast as my dad's trousers could take him. He'd obviously fancied Mum but was not so keen on the idea of her having kids.

I noticed Mum was flustered and distracted that evening. In fact, that might have been when she started checking for wrinkles in the mirror. Then she went back to normal until a week or so later when she got The Phone Call.

"How did you get our number? Directory Inquiries? Oh, wow! No, don't worry. I don't think you're a stalker or anything. Actually, I'm *glad* you phoned. . . ."

And that was that. Yellow Tie Man came into our lives.

But hopefully, he won't be around much longer. I know

I can use my skills to bring Mum to her senses and get her priorities straight.

She needs to see Stuart for what he is. He may seem like a relaxed and (according to Loops) attractive person who adores her, but in actual fact, he is a yellow knitted tie–wearing, TV-hating ecofascist.

Once she realizes this, she'll soon switch from Smitten Mode to Irritated Mode. Then, once she dumps him, I can get her back to Happy Mode and everything will be back to what it was before. Easy! It will be mode-switching at its best!

Sunday, August 16: 6:05 p.m.

◎ STOP THE PRESSES! ◎

I've just accidentally come across something very interesting. I was looking for my hairbrush, which I thought had rolled under the bed, when I found an old shoe box wrapped in one of Mandy's sweatshirts.

As soon as I opened it I realized it was full of Mandy's special stuff—there were a couple of photos of Dad, and birthday cards he'd given her, and the bunny rattle she had when she was a baby.

I felt a bit guilty looking at her private stuff. I was about to shut the lid and put it back when I caught sight of a piece of paper. Written in Mandy's very best script was the following:

Mrs. Joshua Weston

Mandy Weston

Amanda Weston

Mrs. J. Weston

Mrs. Amanda Weston

Mr. and Mrs. Joshua Weston

Dr. and Mrs. Weston

Dr. and Dr. Weston

The Doctors Weston

Joshua Weston is Loops's big brother!!! Mandy likes him!!!!!!!!!!!!!!! Ha! Ha! Ha! This is brilliant! She's always so rude to him. Everybody thinks she hates him, but she loves him!!!!! This is *so good*. It's the absolute best thing that's happened to me all week.

The Doctors Weston is the best. It must be Mandy's fantasy—the two of them in matching white coats with stethoscopes. Which is *hilarious,* as Mandy is rubbish at biology; I think she even fainted one time when they were dissecting something. Obviously Mandy's been watching far too many hospital dramas.

I can't believe Mandy is also in Smitten Mode! How weird that she could even be thinking about marrying some-one. She's definitely developing more and more Grown-Up tendencies. Very worrying.

Joshua Weston's hair is not as red as Loops's; it's more strawberry blond. He scowls most of the time, probably because his parents are always fighting about taking the garbage out.

He's got *no idea* that Mandy likes him, since she's so *horrible* to him! It must be her way of paying him attention . . . but it seems to have backfired. He thinks she hates him! So he's hardly going to ask her out, is he?

Hee, hee, hee! I *can't wait* till she gets home.

10:57 p.m.

When Mandy finally got in tonight I confronted her, in a very mature manner, by waving the list in front of her face and chanting, "Mandy loves Joshua! Ha-ha! Ha-ha!"

I have *never* seen Mandy so angry. She instantly overheated. She was definitely not her usual "I'm so cool because I'm fifteen" self. In fact, for a while she seemed unable to catch her breath! Probably because she knew I'd been looking through her precious shoe box. If only it was that easy to switch Mum's modes these days!

When she recovered herself, Mandy told me that if I breathe a word of what I'd learned to a living soul, she'll tell everyone in Brindleton (possibly by going door to door) that I still wet the bed! Which is not true, by the way, in case you are wondering. But there is *no way* I'm squealing.

After that was decided, we did have a little talk about

it. Apparently she hasn't even told the Clones that she likes Joshua. She's terrified they'd tell him and then he'd laugh at her.

"But you're not ugly or weird or anything," I said. "Why would he laugh at you?"

"I don't know," she muttered, "but it would be just my luck. Anyway, if I tell Lucy and the others I like him, they'll joke that we'll have angry-looking babies."

"But Joshua doesn't glare all the time, it's just when he's around his family!" I protested.

"You know what they're like," she said. And she's right. The Clones can be so *mean* to each other! I'm glad me and Hannah and Loops don't do that.

It feels good talking to Mandy and knowing something the Clones don't. It feels more like being sisters again. Even if she is prepared to tell the world terrible lies about me.

Tuesday, August 18: 9:00 p.m.

 ## FANCYING THE PANTS OFF MODE

Fancying the Pants Off Mode is the mode Grown-Ups employ when they have a massive crush on someone—usually some celebrity on TV, but occasionally some unfortunate real person. Fancying the Pants Off means they fancy someone so much that they wish that person's pants were literally off, which means they wish they could see their bum—very rude. This is **COMPLETELY DISGUSTING** and should be discouraged.

I have put my mode-switching plan into action. I am sitting on the sofa with Mum and Mandy, writing this while watching this old eighties film called *Moonstruck* for about the millionth time. It's Mum's favorite film, because she fancies the pants off Nicolas Cage. There's a scene in it—which is just coming up, actually—where Nicolas Cage says, "Love isn't meant to be good, it's meant to break your heart!" and goes on to give this big speech about how people love the wrong people.

Mum loves that bit and knows it by heart. It's so funny to see her saying all the words—especially as there's a bit where he says "Now I want you to get upstairs, and **GET INTO MY BED!**" That bit gets Mum very excited. So she is obviously imagining getting between the sheets with old Cagey-Boy. **EUEEEEERGH!**

When Mum and Auntie Julie talk about Nicolas Cage and Gary Barlow, they say, "I wouldn't kick him out of bed."

Does that mean that other men, who are not Gary Barlow or Nicolas Cage, are constantly getting kicked out of bed? There must be a lot of men sleeping on floors out there.

Going back to *Moonstruck,* I'm sure being reminded of how much she fancies Nicolas Cage and hearing that speech about people loving the wrong people will convince her that Stuart is not at all hot—*and* all wrong for her!

My skills in the operation of Grown-Ups are as strong as ever. Mum's *definitely* going to stay in more now. I told her that Jack had a little cry when I was putting him to bed two weekends ago because he missed her so much. Well, his eyes *were* watering, as he was laughing so much about eating boogers. So that is, technically, crying. I'm not a complete Filthy Dirty Liar.

Making your Grown-Up feel guilty is just another operational technique that helps you stay in control. Use it wisely.

You should have seen Mum's face. She might as well have had "guilty" tattooed all over her forehead. We'll *definitely* be having more nights like this, just us together. Perfect results!

Talking of "Fancying the Pants Off," I don't think Hannah is as committed to Ben Clayden as she pretends to be. It's all "Neil this" and "Neil that" these days. I think she's secretly liked him for ages. He'll probably ask her out and then they'll eventually have to kiss. That's what's expected when you go out with someone. Thomas Finch certainly didn't have a clue about that part of the deal—he didn't even speak to me, let alone kiss me. And to be honest, I was sort of relieved about that . . . not the not-speaking bit, but the not-kissing bit.

The truth is I don't have a clue about kissing. Which could mean major embarrassment should the occasion arise before I die. Mandy and the Clones have all done it. In fact, they seem to do nothing else. Even though she loves Joshua Weston, it doesn't stop Mandy from randomly kissing people from her class at school just as much as all the other Clones do. They treat it like a hobby.

Hannah and Loops and me discussed the subject on Hannah's garage roof earlier, where we were sunbathing.

"Do you know how to kiss properly? Like a French kiss?" I asked them.

"Well I've not done it *properly,* if that's what you mean," said Hannah, "but I think you sort of do this. . . ."

Then she held up her right hand and made a fake mouth out of her first finger curled over and her thumb. She proceeded to pretend to kiss it, which involved moving her head from side to side and doing a sort of goldfish thing with her mouth.

"Hannah, have you been practicing with your *hand*??!!" cried Loops. Loops and me started rolling around, laughing. My stomach was actually aching. Hannah looked hurt.

"So are you the experts, then?" she said sarcastically.

"Honestly, I haven't a clue." Which made us all laugh even more. Hannah and Loops know that when I was supposed to be going out with Thomas Finch, we were rarely in the same room. In fact, it's a bit of a running joke—my non-relationship. Sometimes I wonder if we ever did actually go out with each other, or if I just imagined it.

"*I've* had a proper kiss," said Loops casually.

"What? And you never told us?" said Hannah, sitting bolt upright, outraged.

"It was only last week." Loops smiled to herself. "And I needed some time . . . to think about it all."

I rolled over and pointed an imaginary gun to her head. "Well, go on, who was it? If you don't tell us, we'll have to kill you!"

"It was with Jonathan Elliott!" said Loops. "I met him at the park and we sat in the teenagers' shelter for ages. He was telling me about the universe and how small Earth is. Apparently Earth is like this tiny, microscopic speck compared to our sun, and our sun is this even more microscopic dot compared to some *other* sun called Antares!"

"It sounds fascinating. . . ," I couldn't resist saying. I must stop being so sarcastic.

"**SHUT UP!** Let her finish!" shouted Hannah, who was unreasonably excited.

"It's odd," said Loops, "but what he said about how microscopic Earth is and how we're like this speck of dust in this huge universe freaked me out big-time. So he put his arm round me and said he was sorry if he'd upset me. I thought he was being nice, but suddenly he started kissing me!"

"You didn't want him to?" I said, ready to be enormously indignant on her behalf.

"I did, but I didn't expect him to do a big French kiss straightaway. I thought we might do some smaller ones first. I think he did lots of kissing with some girl he met last summer on holiday, so he definitely knows how."

"Did you like it?" asked Hannah.

"Sort of. I think I'd get used to it," said Loops, looking uncharacteristically thoughtful.

"So, are you going out with him?" I asked.

"No. He asked me if we could meet up again, but I said no. I like him, but I think he's too experienced for me. It made me feel like a beginner."

"Well, he's a huge know-it-all about everything else!" I said. "He's probably got a book at home called *Advanced Kissing Techniques*."

"It wasn't like that," said Loops, still looking slightly wistful. "I just don't think I'm ready right now. I told him to ask me out again in a few months."

So Loops has been kissed!!! I wonder who'll be next. Part of me thinks it's all pretty disgusting. Maybe that's because of Jack. His definition of kissing is "when teenagers lick the insides of each other's mouths." Now, that's enough to put anyone off for life.

When you think of it that way, being a bald, toothless, bearded nun in the Himalayas with only a donkey for a friend is suddenly quite appealing.

Got sunburned, and despite *buckets* of after-sun lotion, my nose is bright red. I look so hideously mutant, I guarantee that tomorrow I will bump into the person I "Fancy the Pants Off"—Ben Clayden.

Wednesday, August 19: 2:05 p.m.

ANGRY MODE

Angry Mode is pretty self-explanatory. Be aware that if your Grown-Up is in Stressed or Grumpy Mode, they can easily switch to Angry Mode with hardly any intervention from you. Avoiding your Grown-Up until they have cooled down is the only option you should consider. Any other courses of action are dangerous.

!WARNING

Angry Mode can lead (if you push your Grown-Up to extremes) to short-circuiting and in some cases complete meltdown. This should be avoided, as it can seriously impair function.

Mum went into Angry Mode this morning, which is not at all like her. Yet again, this shows how unpredictable she's becoming. I blame Stuart. Not for any good reason; I just feel like it.

We were at the minimart doing our big weekly shop, so

{106}

she was being hassled like always. I was moaning loudly about my red sunburned nose, while Mandy and Jack were trying to get her to buy them magazines. It was a normal shopping trip, not something that would have ever tipped her into Angry Mode before.

As usual, Mum told Mandy and Jack in no uncertain terms that magazines were not part of our grocery budget. Nan was behind the counter nearby, serving customers. She shouted over, "Quite right, Alison. Don't give in, they're trying it on!"

Then Auntie Sarah (one of Mum's cousins—the one who's married to Scary Uncle Alan from the Gregg family) walked in with my Archenemy, Leanne, and her older sister, Shannon, who is like Leanne but worse. Leanne and Shannon went straight over to the magazines and Auntie Sarah let them each get one.

☹ SAD BUT TRUE FACT

Some Grown-Ups say yes more easily than others.

"Mu-um, Auntie Sarah's letting them get their magazines as part of *their* grocery shop!" shouted Jack. He'd already spent his pocket money on sweets, but he was so greedily desperate to get a *Doctor Who* magazine he was willing to try anything.

"Well, I'm not Auntie Sarah!" said Mum, who was starting to display signs of Stressed Mode.

"What do you mean by *that*?" said Auntie Sarah, who may only be a Gregg by marriage but has most of the Gregg-like scary qualities.

"What I mean by that," said Mum, "is they've spent their pocket money and I don't get them magazines, that's all. Do you have a problem or something?"

Mum is not one who is easily bullied.

"It sounded like you were making a point—'*I'm* not Auntie Sarah.'" Auntie Sarah was nose to nose with Mum by this point. Both Mandy and Jack had flung their magazines back on the shelves and were trying to avoid the smug "I've got a magazine and you don't" stares from Leanne and Shannon. For once I was off the hook. I was hiding behind the potato chip rack.

"Take it like that if you want," said Mum, "I've got enough on my plate."

"So I hear," said Auntie Sarah with a sniff.

"What's *that* supposed to mean?" We could see Mum bristling.

"Your new boyfriend," said Auntie Sarah. "It must be using up a lot of your energy, dragging up your kids *and* going out with a boy toy."

There was a horrible, horrible silence. Part of me was annoyed on Mum's behalf, but I have to admit that another part was thinking, *This is just what Mum needs to hear! This is how people see her and Stuart.*

Over at the counter, Nan was holding a bag of sugar in the air, suspended between where she'd scanned it and the shopping bag it was supposed to go in.

I came out from behind the crisps rack and saw, to my absolute horror, that Ben Clayden was in the doorway of the shop and had heard *everything*. Not only that, he also saw my luminous neon-red clown's nose.

This had to be the worst day of my life. Leanne and Shannon sniggered nastily.

"Look," said Leanne, pointing at me, "Christmas must be coming early. Rudolph's here!"

"Come on, you lot," said Mum, now in full Angry Mode and pushing past Auntie Sarah, "we haven't got all day to listen to people talking rubbish."

We went round the shop in record time, throwing stuff into the shopping cart. This is how we shop normally, to be honest, Mum does not enjoy shopping—well, not the boring shopping for food and essentials anyway.

I ran behind Mum and the trolley with my head down, hoping I wouldn't have to see Ben Clayden again. Of course I saw him again at least twice, and each time ducked my head even lower. Jack's always going on about wishing he had an invisibility cloak like Harry Potter. Now I understand what he means.

There's usually a long line in the morning. Everyone in our town seems to like to grocery shop mid-week. By the time we got to the front, Auntie Sarah and Leanne and Shannon had joined the end of it.

"Are you all right, Alison?" Nan said as she loaded up the two big cotton bags Stuart's given Mum so we won't waste plastic bags. They have *Save the Environment* printed on the side. Another daily reminder of his interfering do-goodery.

"Fine," said Mum through gritted teeth. I knew she was very angry because her knuckles were white from where she was gripping her purse.

Nan winked.

"People in glass houses shouldn't throw stones," she said.

"Yes," said Mum loudly, "you're absolutely right there!"

Auntie Sarah drew in her breath as if to speak, but seemed to think better of it. Nobody messes with Nan. I laughed. Leanne glared straight at me. I'll pay for it when we go back to school, but right then I couldn't have cared less.

When we left the shop, Mum was still mad. I could tell we would be in for a bad day if we didn't get her out of Angry Mode quick. I was racking my brains to think of what I could do or say, when Jack solved the problem. He said exactly the right thing.

"You know how we've been studying animals of Africa at school, Mum? Well, when I saw the picture of a warthog I thought, *That's Auntie Sarah!*"

"Jack!" said Mum. "You mustn't say such rude things about people."

But I could see that she was pleased.

4:15 p.m.

It normally takes a lot for Mum to switch to Angry Mode, or to overheat. And she's always easy to switch out of it. The secret is to make her laugh, and Dad was an expert at that.

I remember the time Dad went to a work colleague's bachelor party and did not come home *all night*. He stayed over at Uncle Kevin's but didn't phone to tell Mum. Mum was only able to stay angry till teatime the next day, when Dad went and sat in Rascal's tiny dog basket with a very funny sad expression on his face. When he stood up, the basket was wedged onto his bum, so of course she couldn't help laughing.

We haven't seen Stuart angry yet. I've only ever seen him being happy. It would be great if it turns out that he's got a rage problem and becomes a monster. Then Mum would dump him double quick because she's not the type to put up with that.

I wonder if he'd get angry if we did something environmentally unfriendly. It would be great for Mum to see an unpleasant side to perfect Stuart. A reality check, if you like.

It's important to know what Grown-Ups are like when they get angry; it tells you a lot about them. Will Stuart wave his hands about and shout? Or will he go quiet? We'll have to find out. He can't stay happy forever, not if he's got anything to do with our family. Got to go now to ask Mandy.

5:05 p.m.

I've just had a conversation with Mandy about the doing-something-environmentally-unfriendly idea. She thinks it's a great plan, so when Stuart is over next we're going to abuse the new recycling system he set up for Mum. Instead of putting paper and plastic in the green recycling bin, we'll put it in the trash bin like we used to. That'll show him!

11:34 p.m.

Mum decided to stay in tonight with us! It was just like old times—snuggled up on the sofa, watching TV and chatting. Obviously Auntie Sarah's words hit a nerve. She helped me put tons of calamine lotion on my nose—it stinks. It had better work. Otherwise my nose will be in Angry Mode all week.

Sunday, August 23

DOING SOMETHING NICE MODE

Most Grown-Ups periodically switch into Doing Something Nice Mode, mainly when they feel that they need to add some luxury or excitement or variety to their dull and hopeless lives. Usually this involves them planning something, making an effort and finally enjoying whatever it is they planned and made an effort for. The more planning and making an effort involved, the more determined the Grown-Ups will be to enjoy themselves.

Mum's been in Doing Something Nice Mode all day. I don't think it's because she wants to add excitement or variety to her life—I think it's more to do with her feeling bad about neglecting us for her new boyfriend. So not only did she stay in with us last night, today she's decided to cook us all a "lovely meal." Doing Something Nice Mode is always Mum's way of saying sorry. Of course, she's spoiling it by inviting the very person we don't want around.

To make matters worse, there's the small matter of Mum's cooking. . . .

COOKING MODE

One of the main purposes and functions of Grown-Ups is to keep you fed. We're already at their mercy when it comes to stuff like pocket money and lifts to places. Grown-Ups control the quality of your diet, which is fundamental to your health, but it's potluck whether you get healthy food or junk food packed with killer fats. Which is quite serious, actually, when you think about it.

If your Grown-Up has a *malfunction* in their Cooking Mode there's not much you can do except:

1) Eat their cooking and risk death.

2) Learn to cook yourself by watching one of the twenty thousand shows on TV that tell you how.

3) Live on takeout, doughnuts and crisps and end up on a documentary called FAT BRITAIN: PEOPLE WHO HAVE TO BE LIFTED OUT OF THEIR HOUSES WITH CRANES.

Dad used to do the cooking in our house—proper meals like shepherd's pie and roast dinners, since Mum wasn't very interested and he enjoyed it. When Mum had to take over after he died, it was difficult for her. She'd be in the kitchen slaving away for hours to make these horrible meals. Nobody had the heart to tell her how disgusting her food was. In fact, we'd all try to cheer her up by telling her that what she'd made was delicious.

The problem is we were too enthusiastic and we've made her think she's actually *good* at it. And that has made things a hundred times worse, because now she's decided she's far too brilliant to have to follow recipes. Which is why, half an hour ago, me and Mandy offered to take over. But Mum wouldn't hear of it. She believes that she has talent in the kitchen, thanks to our Filthy Dirty Lying.

☹ SAD BUT TRUE FACT

If you tell a Grown-Up that they are good at something, even if they are not, *they will believe it*. This applies to cooking, dancing, singing and many other things. Be careful what you tell them. You know those talentless Grown-Ups who appear on the early auditions of televised talent shows? Somebody out there, probably their children, told them that they were fantastic.

Regarding this cooking business, I have to admit that I have totally and miserably failed in the operation of my Grown-Up. I still don't have the heart to tell Mum the truth and neither does Mandy, who is actually a big softie under her "couldn't care less" exterior. Maybe one day we'll find the courage.

So that's why right now Mum is concocting something out of various tins and packets and Jack is setting the table nicely. See? *Another* change—normally we eat in front of the **TV**!

Stuart is bound to show up soon, and then he'll probably stay all evening. You know my masterstroke of getting Mum to stay in more by cranking up the guilt about Jack? Well, it's backfired, because now they're *both* staying in. He's been coming round **LOADS** and is a permanent fixture in my usual spot on the sofa next to Mum!

And guess what? Rascal has proved himself to be a **MAJOR** traitor! He jumps up on Stuart's lap and snuggles up to him! It's a bit upsetting, really, because he used to do that with Dad. Dad picked Rascal out from the animal shelter when I was five. And this is how Rascal thanks him, by betraying his memory!

Rascal's judgment is obviously just as bad as Mum's.

11:32 p.m.

I wish I could say that the "Doing Something Nice" was actually nice. Unfortunately, it was about as far from it as you can imagine. It was a disaster.

Stuart got here at about five o'clock, and Mum served up one of her famous "Oh My God What Is This" stews.

We sat down and—like soldiers going to war—battled our way through our dinner. It was particularly disgusting. I'm not sure what it was, but I think there were raisins in it. Stuart had brought a bottle of red wine. He certainly needed it, to wash down her horrible food. He must really like her, to stick around and eat what she serves up.

I got out the bread so I could fill up on bread and butter, as usual.

Halfway through the meal, Mum cleared her throat and looked around at all of us, with a big bright smile on her face. This gave away the fact that she was nervous about what she was going to say.

"I've got some news!" she said. "Stuart and I are thinking of going on a mini-break!"

We looked at her blankly. Then—as the awful truth sank in—I realized that Mum wasn't in Doing Something Nice Mode for *us* at all. She didn't feel bad about neglecting us. She wasn't even sorry. This whole cooking a special meal was just to butter us up so we'd be fine about her doing something nice *with Yellow Tie Man!* Not that what she's planning is nice. *Far from it.*

A mini-break is a weekend away for Grown-Ups where they do lots of cuddling.

I know this sad but true fact because I've seen this film called *Bridget Jones's Diary*. In fact, I watched it with Mum. And here she was boasting about planning one, in front of her children.

Mandy's face was clouding over. I know that look, and it's not good. It means she could switch to full-on Angry Mode at any moment. Mum saw it too, but she carried on.

"We're thinking of going to Barcelona! Stuart is going to show me the architecture. It's supposed to be spectacular!"

Jack looked confused.

"So you're going all that way to look at an architecture?" he asked. "What's an architecture?"

"Architecture is the way different buildings are designed—" began Stuart enthusiastically.

"Yes, Jack," interrupted Mandy sarcastically, "that's *all* they will be doing from first thing in the morning to last thing at night. Walking round Barcelona for three days looking at buildings . . . over and over and over again."

Mum glared at Mandy.

"Cool," said Jack, and carried on eating.

I decided to try to be gracious about it, but halfway through I couldn't help it, I had to make a little jibe. I mean, when's the last time we got to go on holiday? Not since the trip to Bognor last summer with Auntie Susan, Uncle Dave, Hannah and Matthew.

"I hope you have a really amazing time," I said. "I'd *love* the chance to go somewhere exciting."

"We've *never been abroad*," Mandy whispered very loudly to Stuart. It's true. When we were little, Mum and Dad were too broke. Then Dad was ill, and since then we've done British holidays, usually with relatives. Gale-force winds, sitting on beaches in the rain eating sand-filled egg sandwiches, that sort of thing.

I wondered how she was planning to pay for this mini-break . . . and then it occurred to me. Our Rainy Day money!

The silence was deafening.

"I'll help," said Stuart, getting to his feet. Mandy was already clearing up in a martyr-like way.

"Thanks," said Mum. She knew she couldn't say anything that wouldn't make things worse. I felt bad. Having been in Happy Mode when she told us the news, now she looked disappointed and tired.

"You're doing a great job there," said Stuart to Mandy.

Mandy did not reply, but pointedly picked up the empty plastic bread bag and put it in the normal trash bin, looking straight at Stuart! I saw Stuart flinch, but he didn't say anything. Mandy caught my eye and signaled for "upstairs."

Within minutes, me, Mandy and Jack were again in the Cupboard, having our second Council of War.

"What nerve!" said Mandy. "She's turning into one of those mums who goes on holiday and leaves their kids at home alone. We should phone Social Services."

"That's a *bit* harsh," I said, "but you know what this means? It means they've moved on to the second stage of their relationship. A mini-break is like a test to see if they can spend a lot of time together without wanting to kill each other. If they can get through a mini-break, they know that they could live together!"

Mandy looked horrified.

"I wouldn't mind if Stuart lives in our house," said Jack matter-of-factly. "He's okay. He gave me a piggy bank."

"Jack, you can't think that someone's okay just because they give you a cool piggy bank!" said Mandy. "If Adolf Hitler gave you a new piggy bank would you think he was okay?"

"Yes," said Jack. "Who's Adolf Hitler?"

MIDNIGHT

Yes, it's official. I can't sleep due to Mum's latest major malfunction. Mandy doesn't seem so bothered, she's snoring away like a water buffalo. Charming. Before she went to sleep, she agreed with me that we can't count on Jack to help us in our campaign to get rid of Stuart.

"Do you think he noticed that I didn't recycle?" Mandy asked.

"Definitely," I said. "I think he got the message. From now on we should *never* recycle when he's around."

"Good idea," said Mandy. "What else can we do?"

This felt good, my big sister consulting me for tips on how to annoy Stuart. I racked my brains. Now was my chance to show my expertise, my vast skills in the operation of Grown-Ups.

"I know," I said at last. "You know how he hates advertising and he wears that 'No Logo' T-shirt all the time? I think we need to get branded up!"

"Katie," said Mandy in admiration, "you're an Evil Genius!"

"I know," I said. Sometimes you have to admit you've got what it takes.

Tuesday, August 25

 WORRIED MODE

Grown-Ups go into Worried Mode when things are not going the way they want them to—especially if this means you or they will be in danger, or not be safe and secure.

Grown-Ups can also switch to Worried Mode when they feel that people are criticizing them or are angry or annoyed with them.

I just walked into the kitchen, and Mum's looking really worried. She's just been on the phone with Gran Sutton, who's told her not to bother coming to the lunch she invited us to the other week. We are definitely not in her good book.

I think it's due to Gran Sutton's not being happy about Mum seeing Stuart. After all, Dad was her son, and now Mum's got this younger man on the go. I've stopped calling him Yellow Tie Man now. I've joined Mandy in calling him the Boy Toy.

Now Mum's on the phone with Auntie Julie. She's trying to get reassurance probably. Seeing as we all live in Brindle-ton, family is pretty important.

Of course, all the aunts and uncles and cousins don't get along all the time, but we know we can rely on each other. I don't know what we'd have done without everyone after Dad died. Auntie Susan and Uncle Dave were brilliant. Probably because not only is Auntie Susan my mum's sister, but Uncle Dave's my dad's brother—which technically makes me and Hannah double cousins! Which is cool, though probably not that unusual in a place like Brindleton.

We ate dinner almost every night at Auntie Susan and Uncle Dave's house for months and months, until Mum decided that she was going to throw herself into cooking tons of things.

Even now, Mum can lift the phone and mention to Uncle Pete or Uncle Kevin that a cupboard door needs fixing and they'll be round that night. And if anyone needs our help, we're there for them too. We all look out for one another. It's a good feeling.

So it would be no joke if there was some sort of family feud thanks to the Boy Toy. Which is another reason why it would be best for everyone if Mum dumped him.

Plus Mum can't even talk to Stuart about all the trouble he's causing. He has a very strange attitude about family. I know his parents live in Oxford somewhere, but he always changes the subject if you ask too many questions. Mum told us he doesn't have any brothers or sisters.

The other day, I asked him when he was next going to visit his mum and dad.

"Maybe around Christmas," he said.

"When did you last see them?" I asked.

"Easter, I think," he replied. It was *so weird*! It was as if he thought it was normal to go and see your parents, who live *really close to you,* twice a year! Even Mum looked slightly surprised by that one.

"Don't you *like* them?" asked Jack. We can always rely on Jack to get straight to the point.

Stuart looked embarrassed.

"Of course I do," he said, and then he went really quiet.

Something about his tone of voice made us not want to ask any more. I can imagine Stuart's poor mum and dad sitting waiting for him to visit them. But he's too busy visiting us to give them a moment's thought. And to think Great-Grandma Peters feels neglected!

I'll just have to leave Mum with her worries for now; I'm planning on going into Oxford with Hannah. It's just the two of us, as Loops is doing a gymnastics competition. But Mum's asked me to take Jack to the library first, because he wants some Asterix books, so I've got to hurry.

11:00 a.m.

I am just back from the library and am rushing even more to get ready for the Oxford trip . . . but I **HAD** to write down what's just happened. There I was in the library with Jack, telling him to hurry up and choose an Asterix book or I'd kick him in the bum, when who should walk into the library but Thomas Finch!

He didn't see us, and can you guess what he did? He went straight over to the Romance section and picked out about ten Mills & Boon books!!!!!!!

"Hello, Thomas!" I said casually, strolling over. "I didn't know you were a Mills and Boon fan. . . ."

He went absolutely beetroot under his tan.

"They—they're for my mum," he stammered. "She's got the flu."

"Yes, I'm sure they are!" I said, with what I hoped was a knowing smile. "Come on, Jack, we've got to go!"

3:56 p.m.

Had the *best* trip to Oxford with Hannah. We had burgers, then went up to Oxford Castle and spent about an hour drinking one cup of coffee each and watching people come and go. Some of those international exchange students—the ones over learning English as a foreign language—are almost as good-looking as Ben Clayden. Then we went to all our favorite shops, I didn't buy anything, but Hannah got a belt.

On the bus ride home, I told Hannah about Thomas and the romance books.

"I don't think they're for his mum at all," I said. "I bet he reads them every night."

Hannah dissolved into giggles.

"That's harsh, Katie," she managed to get out. "And I thought you liked him."

Why did she think that? I don't fancy him at all. Well, maybe I do a bit. But why on earth would I want to go out with someone who can't talk to me and whose favorite book is *Love Under the Lonely Moonlight*?

Hannah gets some weird ideas in her head.

4:30 p.m.

Mum's in the kitchen right now having a cup of tea with Auntie Susan. They've decided that Mum's going to host lunch at our house on Saturday so that Auntie Julie and

Auntie Susan and Uncle Dave can meet Stuart properly. This is obviously a reaction to Gran Sutton's disapproval.

This plan seems to have cheered Mum up slightly, although I think she still looks worried. I don't like her being in Worried Mode. Worried Mode can lead to Stressed or even Sad Mode, and neither of those is good.

◎ STRESSED MODE ◎

When Grown-Ups are in Stressed Mode you have to watch out, because they get all uptight about stuff they don't normally care about.

It's best to treat Stressed Mode in a similar way to Grumpy or Angry Mode and use the Avoidance Technique. Whatever you do, don't suggest to them that they should "chillax." That is absolutely the worst word you can use when you are around a Grown-Up in Stressed Mode. It is guaranteed to tip them over the edge.

Today has been quite a day.

Mum had this bizarre idea of having a picnic instead of a normal lunch indoors—it's the typically random sort of thing my mum does.

When I got in from Hannah's, Mum was wandering about as usual in the kitchen in Dad's sweater, but I could tell from the way her shoulders were slightly hunched that stress was setting in. So I crept upstairs to the Cupboard, where Mandy was looking uncharacteristically thoughtful while straightening her hair.

"We've got to do something to show Mum he's not good enough for her," she said, without even so much as a hello first.

It was then that I had a brain wave.

"Stuart gets hay fever," I said. "Why don't we mow the lawn while Mum's at the minimart?"

There was a silence while Mandy took it in.

"Genius!" she said.

So while Mum was out buying her picnic ingredients, Mandy and I got to work. It only took five minutes, as our back garden is so small we can't even play swingball in it without hitting our rackets on the fence.

When Mum got back from the shops and saw us putting the lawn mower away, she gave a little yelp. Mums do that sometimes, the sudden yelping.

"You mowed the lawn! I think it might set off Stuart's hay fever!"

"Oh, sorry," I said. "We thought we were helping."

"Never mind," said Mum, putting her arm around me, "you're good girls for wanting to help."

If only she knew.

I had the job of spreading picnic blankets on the newly

mown grass, and of course, I made sure that they got covered in stray clippings we'd not raked up properly.

Stuart turned up first. He and Mum had a great big kiss in the front hall, and I could tell Jack was thinking about the tentacle-faced Ood. He wasn't the only one.

As soon as Stuart went outside he said, "Oh . . . you cut the grass. . . ."

"Stuart, I'm so sorry . . . ," said Mum. "Mandy and Katie forgot about your *hay fever*! They were just trying to help."

Stuart gave me a penetrating look. I wondered if he suspected anything. I could see that his eyes were watering already. He got out a large handkerchief (I mean, who carries handkerchiefs? Boy Scouts and your granddad, that's who) and wiped them and his giant nose, which was beginning to run.

"I'll be okay," he said unconvincingly.

"Well, at least come inside now," said Mum. "You can help me with the drinks."

Mum was making fruit punch, so Mandy was cutting up oranges in the kitchen.

"Hi, Mandy!" said Stuart in his cheerful voice.

Mandy glared at him. Then she continued hacking away at the orange as if she was chopping Stuart's head into pieces. He looked disturbed and glanced at Mum. Mum looked questioningly at Mandy, who continued hacking at the orange with a demented smile on her face. At that moment, the doorbell rang. Mum was by now so massively stressed out she practically leaped into the air.

"Katie, can you get that?" she cried.

I answered the door. It was Auntie Julie, carrying a picnic basket.

"I've brought my own," she whispered. "Thought it was safer."

Auntie Julie was wearing a flowery dress. The trouble was that this one was way too frilly, with bright colors, so it made her look like she was wearing a pair of Nan's curtains.

Auntie Julie is not fat, but she's not thin either. She's "curvy," as my mum puts it, which means that she's got a big bum. This dress made her bum look enormous. I could see Jack staring at it (he couldn't avoid it, it was at his eye level) and I wondered if he was going to make some comment. To my relief he didn't. I didn't say anything, of course; I've learned that honesty is not always appreciated by Grown-Ups, especially if it's about how they look.

"Nice dress, Jules!" trilled Mum, switching easily into

Lying Mode. "Come on through, we're in the kitchen. Would you like a glass of punch?"

Mum was so stressed she really did not seem herself at all. Her voice didn't sound like her own—it was all falsely bright and cheery.

"Lovely!" said Auntie Julie, imitating Mum's false voice and winking at me.

"Hello," said Stuart to Auntie Julie. "Nice weather for it." Then we stood in terrible silence, the sort of silence where everyone is wishing they could think of something to say but can't.

Stuart blew his nose. His eyes were beginning to look bloodshot.

"Have you got a cold?" asked Auntie Julie.

"It's hay fever," said Mum.

"Have you got antihistamines?"

"I don't take them," said Stuart. "I try to only use natural therapies."

Auntie Julie looked disapproving; her mouth tightened, as if she was stopping herself from saying something.

"So, how was your date last night?" Mum hurriedly changed the subject.

"A complete nightmare." Auntie Julie sat down on one

of the kitchen chairs. She seemed exhausted just remembering. "I'd arranged to meet him in the center of Oxford. When I saw him from a distance I turned round and walked in the opposite direction."

"You didn't even introduce yourself?" asked Mum.

"No way! I phoned him from the bus to say I couldn't make it."

"Why didn't you talk to him? He might have been a nice person."

"He was wearing a bobble hat."

"A woolly hat? Well, that can be okay. . . ."

"No, not just a woolly hat. A bobble hat. A woolly hat *with a great big pom-pom on it*."

"Oh."

"Yes. It was the sort of hat very young children wear. *And* it's the middle of summer. . . ."

The doorbell rang again.

"I'll get it!" said Mum, and fled from the kitchen.

We could hear Uncle Dave, Auntie Susan, Hannah and Matthew in the hall, and Mum being super-polite. When they came through, Mum made us all go and sit on the blankets in the garden, as the kitchen was too small for everyone to stand in it.

Mum passed round the punch and then brought out the plates of sandwiches. She went to the kitchen door and shouted to Jack to come back out, as he'd disappeared upstairs.

Auntie Susan had brought her own enormous basket for her family. Which—like Auntie Julie bringing her food—was a bit rude, seeing as Mum had gone to so much trouble. You could see that this was stressing Mum out even more.

The only people forced to eat Mum's sandwiches were me, Mandy, Jack and Stuart, whose nose was now twice its normal size—and remember, it was pretty enormous to start with. His eyes were streaming. I began to feel bad about what I'd done. His whole face was swelling now. Then it occurred to me, what if our earlier actions actually killed him? We would be *murderers*.

"Have you got a cold?" Auntie Susan asked Stuart as she nibbled on a chicken leg. I wished I could swap my beetroot sandwich for it.

"It's allergies," Mum snapped.

"Have you got antihistamines?"

"I don't take them," said Stuart. "I only go for natural remedies when possible."

It was beginning to feel like déjà vu.

Auntie Susan snorted. "Well, a lot of good your natural

remedies are doing you right now. Alison, why don't you get some for him?"

"No, *honestly,* I don't like to take that sort of thing." Stuart looked very uncomfortable, but it was hard to tell if this was because of:

a) his rapidly swelling face, which was making him look like the Elephant Man

b) Auntie Susan not taking no for an answer

c) the tuna and marmalade sandwich he was trying to choke down.

"Oh for goodness' sake! Why don't you **JUST TAKE THE PILLS!**" Mum shouted.

This is what happens with Stressed Mode—all that tension has to come out somehow. Shouting is the typical way with most Grown-Ups, but this was so unlike our mum! Even she looked shocked.

Stuart stared at her in disbelief, looking like a very long-suffering Elephant Man. Nobody knew where to look or what to say. Which just seemed to annoy Mum more.

Thank goodness Jack knows how to fill an awkward silence.

"Auntie Julie," he said, "what does the word 'epic' mean?"

I've since looked it up in the dictionary and it means this:

> ### EPIC (adj.)
>
> 1) Of, constituting, having to do with, or
>   suggestive of a literary epic: an epic poem
> 2) Surpassing the usual or ordinary, particularly
>   in scope or size
> 3) Heroic and impressive in quality

Auntie Julie did not have a dictionary on her, so she did the best she could.

"I'm not completely sure," she said, "but I think it means great, or very big. So big, it's legendary."

"Ah!" said Jack. "So you have an *epic* bum!"

➵ IRRITATED MODE

Irritated Mode is one of those modes that can be a background mode, which means that some Grown-Ups can spend their whole lives being slightly irritated by everything and everyone.

Other Grown-Ups only go into Irritated Mode periodically, usually because of something you've done or said. Certain objects left around the house are guaranteed to trigger

Irritated Mode. For example, most models of Grown-Up will respond strongly to discarded candy wrappers, mold-filled mugs, stale toast, toenail clippings and underpants. Once a certain threshold is reached, Grown-Ups progress to Angry Mode.

After that, the picnic just got worse. Everyone could tell Mum was in Irritated Mode with Stuart. Me, Mandy, Hannah, Jack and Matthew got away as soon as we could. It was awkward sitting there, trying not to stare at Stuart's ever-swelling head.

Me and Hannah decided to go to the park.

"Well, *that* was fun," said Hannah as we walked up the road. "He's made quite an impression!"

"I don't think your mum and dad or Auntie Julie will want to see Mum with someone who'd rather have a giant mutant swollen face than take perfectly good medicine, do you?" I said.

"His face isn't always like that," Hannah pointed out.

"Well, he's always fussy," I muttered. "Natural this, homeopathic that. He obviously doesn't care enough about family to make an effort. Mum *must* see how annoying he is now."

We walked along, enjoying the sunshine and the fact

that we were away from a horrible social situation—mostly of our own making.

"Listen," said Hannah, "before we see Loops, I'd better tell you something. I told Loops you don't like Thomas anymore, so she's going to see if she can get him to ask her out. She wants us to leave her alone with him if we can, so you need to talk to Jonathan and I need to talk to Neil, okay?"

Loops, who, in the last couple of weeks, has kissed Jonathan Elliott but put him "on hold" till she's more "experienced," now wants to get her teeth (or tongue, more appropriately) into Thomas Finch! What a complete hussy!

"Are you okay with that?" Hannah was looking at me oddly.

I linked arms with her. "Course I am!" I said. "I hope she knows she won't get much conversation out of him."

"I don't think it's *conversation* she's interested in," Hannah said with a smirk.

I got a funny feeling when she said that. Sort of resentful and annoyed but at the same time hurt. I told myself to snap out of it.

At the park, Hannah talked to Neil and I talked to Jonathan (who explained the workings of the jet engine to me—oh, please kill me now). Meanwhile, Loops fluttered her eyelashes and chatted to Thomas. He didn't say much. He didn't need to—Loops can talk enough for two. She was twirling her flame-red curls round her finger and looking up into his eyes, giggling and flirting.

Whenever I looked over he seemed to be enjoying the attention.

They even wandered off, over to the teenagers' shelter, the very place where she'd kissed Jonathan. *That must be her lair,* I thought. Like a spider's web, where she catches them, stuns them and eats them. Maybe she'll work her way through all the boys in our class, kissing every one of them in the teenagers' shelter.

Why am I so bothered about what Loops does? It's completely irrational. I mean, it's a free country, isn't it? Loops has every right to practice kissing with anyone she wants to. Maybe I'm just jealous that she's getting more experienced, while I'm still Katie Sutton with the flat chest and the skinny legs who's never been kissed.

"So, the jet engine works on the principle of accelerating a smaller mass of air to a very high velocity," Jonathan was saying, as if he thought I actually cared. He didn't seem bothered by the fact that Loops was chatting up Thomas.

I stared at the sun shining through Jonathan's ears,

thinking how interesting it was that someone who was so earth-shatteringly boring could also be such an accomplished and experienced kisser.

As soon as I could, I made my excuses and went home. I decided it was the perfect time to reorganize my sock drawer. There's something satisfying about sorting out your socks, or maybe I'm just deeply troubled.

8:33 p.m.

So there I was pairing up my pink fluffy slipper socks, when Mandy rushed in and said, "Come and listen to this!" and dragged me to the top of the stairs. We crouched by the banister and listened. Mum and Stuart were having a big fight!

"You should have just taken the medicine," Mum was tutting, in Irritated Mode verging on Angry Mode. "Your eyes nearly swelled shut! You looked *awful*."

"Well, it didn't help sitting in a pile of grass clippings. . . ."

"You didn't talk to Dave. . . ."

"He didn't talk to *me*! He started reading the paper! He did the crossword! And you just talked to your sisters. What was I supposed to do? And I don't think Mandy likes me. She isn't recycling."

"Don't be ridiculous," said Mum, sounding very fed up indeed. "How can you think someone doesn't like you just because they don't recycle? You're being paranoid. Look, I'm not feeling well. I've got a *splitting* headache. I'm going to bed. I think it's time you went home, Stuart."

"Fine," he said abruptly. Shortly afterward we heard the door slam; then Mum gave a big sigh.

If Stuart was an expert in operating Mum, like I am, he would have known that she needs a nice hot chocolate and a head massage to calm her down. But he isn't, and he doesn't. Ha!

This definitely means Mum is no longer in Smitten Mode. It's a major breakthrough.

"I think there's trouble in Paradise," said Mandy cheerfully.

SICK MODE

When your Grown-Up is unwell, do not expect them to perform the same functions as they do normally—this applies equally if they only have a cold or if it's something more serious. Also, do not make too much noise. This can switch them into Grumpy Mode, which is not a good combination with Sick Mode. Handle your sick Grown-Up with care.

Well, we've certainly found out what a whiner Stuart is. Just a few allergies and he was completely pathetic. What would he be like if he was seriously sick like our dad was? Dad was so good-humored, even when he was in loads of discomfort. Mum must see the difference. I'm sure all this will have put her off Stuart for good.

Mum's a lot better at being unwell. She's had to be, as she's been on her own with us for so long and has had to put us first. She's pretty matter-of-fact about illness. She keeps on going until she can't, then goes to bed until she can again, then gets up and gets on with it.

⇨ CARING MODE

Grown-Ups should automatically switch into Caring Mode when you are sick. It's part of their default setting. If your Grown-Up does not do this, then they have a serious malfunction.

I woke up this morning feeling very unwell. My head hurt lots and I didn't want to get up. Part of me thought that it might be karma for what we did to Stuart yesterday. Now I'm going to be ill on the last few days of the last few days of vacation—serves me right.

Around eleven o'clock, Mum came in and took my temperature with the ear thermometer. She went straight into Sympathy Mode and began to perform the Looking After Function—which she's brilliant at.

"Oh dear!" she said. "The thermometer says you're not well. What's hurting?"

"My head, it really hurts," I moaned. Mum went to open the curtains.

"Don't!" I shouted. "It hurts my eyes!"

Of course, I should have realized that this would panic Mum. Sure enough, within the hour Auntie Susan was round prodding and poking at me. She decided that Mum didn't need to rush me to the hospital quite yet and went away while Mum dosed me up with medicine.

Hannah and Loops came and hovered in the door. They had a couple of magazines, but I knew I must be unwell because I didn't even flick through them. I didn't even look at the pages where they show celebrities with cellulite. It had to be serious.

After they left, I imagined Hannah and Loops telling Ben Clayden that I was seriously ill. Perhaps he'll realize that he loves me, despite all the embarrassing things that he's seen me doing, like falling on my chin or hiding behind the potato chip rack in the minimart with a bright red nose. Or that time when Jack burped as we were walking past his house and I'm sure he thought it was me.

Then I wondered what Thomas Finch would think if he heard I was being rushed to the hospital. This is even more ridiculous, since in the last few months I've:

a) dumped him

b) stormed past him

c) laughed at him

d) given my friend permission to chat him up.

So why should I care what he thinks?

2:00 p.m.

Lying in bed with nothing much to do gives you too much time to brood. I found myself thinking about Dad. He was sick for such a long time. He must have been so bored lying there. I wonder what he thought about....

When I was little, I remember Dad would sit me on his knee and give me this great big hug and he'd say:

"Are you beautiful?"

"Yes!"

"Are you a genius?"

"Yes!"

"Are you the bravest?"

"Yes!"

"Are you a sausage?"

I'd scream with laughter at this point.

"No!"

"Are you invincible?"

"Yes!"

"Are you the best?"

"Yes!"

"Are you a smelly old sock?"

I know it sounds stupid, but it was a great game.

Dad was at home for the first six months and then he was in and out of a place called a hospice, which was actually quite good because when he was feeling very bad they made sure he was comfortable.

When he went in we used to visit him lots. At the end he couldn't do anything at all except smile at us. So I suppose you could say that he lost all of his functions and modes in the end, except the Love Mode, which is probably the most important. I think that's why he kept it the longest.

➣ LOVE MODE

Love Mode is different from Smitten Mode. It's an awesome mode, because it makes things better. Well, most of the time, anyway.

Love Mode can be a background mode. This means that even if your Grown-Up has switched to Angry Mode, they can (and usually do) still love you—although this can be hard to detect when they are purple with rage and screaming "Go to your room!"

3:12 p.m.

Mum came in to check on me again. She sat on the bed and stroked my hair.

"Are you feeling better?" she asked.

"Yes, now that *you're* here," I said. "Can I have a cuddle?"

It's pathetic. I mean, I'm thirteen years old. But sometimes you just need a cuddle . . . whatever age you are. She got onto the bed beside me and we snuggled up.

For a while after Dad died, the rest of us all slept together in Mum's bed—all four of us, and sometimes Rascal too. Mum needed millions of hugs. It was a hug extravaganza. I'm glad she needed all those hugs. We needed them too.

I've had so many great Mum hugs today. It's like she's making up for every single hug I've missed since Stuart's been on the scene.

"Love you," she said, "and I'm sorry if I've been distracted recently with Stuart. Have I been neglecting you?"

"You've neglected us massively," I said, smiling to show her I was joking, "but I forgive you. Have you split up with him?"

"I don't know," she said. "I like him, but it's not like

when I started going out with your dad. Things were much easier then. Do you mind me seeing Stuart?"

"No," I lied. "I just want you to be happy."

I *do* want her to be happy. But at the same time, I'm a spoiled brat who doesn't like to share.

7:29 p.m.

Mandy got in a few hours ago, having been up in Oxford with the Clones all day. She bounced into the bedroom remarkably cheerful for a change, carrying a plastic bag.

"I know they might have split up already," she said, "but I got these just in case."

She got out three T-shirts—all branded with giant logos.

"Brilliant!" I said. "We can wear them if he ever dares come back!"

Stuart still hasn't phoned since he left, and Mum says she's not going to phone him. So maybe this is it. Maybe it's over and things can go back to the way they were. Just the four of us. (Or five, if you include Rascal.)

Monday, August 31

I felt better this morning, but not well enough to go rushing about doing things. So I just hung around the house, reading the magazines Hannah and Loops left and watching daytime TV. In sixty years I'll probably end up like Great-Grandma Peters, waving my walking stick at the TV and swearing. Unless, as I'm sure Stuart thinks will happen, we're all living in some sort of wasteland eating poisoned turnips because of global warming.

Hannah and Loops were allowed to visit this afternoon, and they filled me in on what I've been missing. Which of course wasn't much, this being Brindleton. Although there was one significant piece of news.

"You won't believe this," said Loops excitedly. "Joshua's going out with Jenny Caulfield! We saw them walking along holding hands."

I immediately felt gutted for Mandy, but nobody knows, so I couldn't say anything.

After they'd gone I did some thinking about broken hearts.

A NOTE ABOUT BROKEN PARTS

There are no decent spare parts available for your Grown-Up, so careful operation is essential. For example, a broken heart can be very difficult to mend. Sometimes it breaks in two, and sometimes it shatters into a thousand pieces.

Do not attempt major operations, such as heart transplants, yourself. Hospitals are the best places for such overhauls of your Grown-Up, and doctors are quite good at general repairs and maintenance. It is best to leave the technical details to the experts.

When Dad died, Mum's heart was broken into a thousand pieces, and I really did wish I could take her to the hospital and get the doctors to mend it. I wished a team of surgeons would rush in wearing green gowns and make it all better with a bypass or a replacement valve.

But life's not as simple as that.

I wonder how Mum is really feeling about Stuart now that it's over. I don't think she's brokenhearted. Perhaps a couple of small dents, but nothing like she was after Dad.

6:20 p.m.

The phone rang downstairs a while ago, and I can just *tell* it's Stuart. Mum's been talking to him for ages, in a hushed voice. I can't make out what she's saying, but I can hear her laughing.

I can feel my heart sinking.

8:27 p.m.

Ten minutes ago, while I was doing my "cleanse, tone and moisturize" routine (so as to be beautiful enough to be the future Mrs. Clayden), Mandy came home. I could tell she'd heard about Joshua Weston and Jenny Caulfield just from the way she walked into the room.

"Are you all right?" I asked.

"Don't want to talk about it," she said, throwing down her bag and climbing up into the top bunk.

I wish I could get that team of surgeons to mend Mandy's heart, because I know it's broken. I wish I could say something to her that would help. But nothing would. Not right now.

Wednesday, September 2

A NOTE ON ANGRY MODE AND TEENAGERS

Teenagers need more careful handling than Grown-Ups because when they get into Angry Mode, they take it to a whole new level. As with Grown-Ups, the most effective strategy is the Avoidance Technique. Your safety could depend on it.

I know this is supposed to be a guide on Grown-Ups but I thought I would mention this as Mandy has been in Angry Mode since Monday and she's still going strong! First she found out about Joshua and Jenny; then she realized that Mum and Stuart had made up. She's been impossible to talk to ever since. And since I've already noted the danger of younger siblings ruining your plans, I thought I should also make you aware about older siblings. I'm sure Mandy is going to make Mum overheat any second. . . .

If anyone so much as asks Mandy if she wants a cup of tea, she'll turn on them like some sort of wild, angry beast. So I'm using the Avoidance Technique.

The way I've done this is to practically move into Hannah's house, which is how I've been roped into Hannah's latest scheme. It's part of her plan to save the world by raising money for charity. Me and Loops have been helping her on and off all summer.

Today, Hannah had the brilliant idea to sell some of the vegetables from Granddad Williams's garden.

"We can tell him later," she said. "He won't mind."

So we dug up lots of potatoes, carrots and rhubarb and took them back to Hannah's house in Uncle Dave's wheelbarrow. When all the vegetables were washed, we put them back in the wheelbarrow but arranged them more artistically. Then we wheeled it along to the same street as the minimart, but about fifty meters down from it.

Loops made a sign saying: POTATOES. CARROTS. RHUBARB. ALL PROCEEDS TO CHILDREN IN AFRICA.

Then we waited for the money to roll in. But it didn't. Nobody seemed interested, until at last Creepy Mr. Cooper came along and bought a big load of carrots, probably just to be kind.

"I'll be like Bugs Bunny when I eat this lot!" he joked. We laughed hysterically.

"I might just have a few of those potatoes as well," he said. I picked some up, ready to hand them to him.

At that moment, Nan came out of the minimart to smoke a cigarette and she saw us. She came charging along and shouted, "What's this then? Have you got a vendor's license?"

"But it's for charity!" I protested.

"And the road to hell is paved with good intentions! That lot had better not be from our plot!"

Then I noticed that Hannah and Loops hadn't stopped to argue—they were halfway down the road with the wheelbarrow! And Creepy Mr. Cooper had run off with his carrots. This is because everybody in the whole of Brindleton is afraid of Nan Williams. Including me. She really is terrifying when she's in Angry Mode.

I ran after Hannah and Loops but was slowed down since I was still holding Creepy Mr. Cooper's potatoes. Then, as I rounded the corner, I bumped straight into Thomas Finch. I dropped the potatoes, which rolled all over the pavement.

"Sorry!" I said, and started to pick them up. I expected him to help me. He's the sort of person who'd usually do that. Only he didn't. He watched me scrabbling about on the ground.

"Had a laugh, have you?" he said, glaring down at me.

I looked up, puzzled. "What do you mean?"

"You think it's so funny: 'Thomas Finch was at the library with a pile of Mills and Boon books. He must love reading romance novels!'"

I stood up, feeling terrible, with my armful of stolen potatoes. Hannah must have said something to Neil Parkhouse.

"Listen, I'm sorry. I didn't mean—"

"I only went to get some library books for my mum, who had the flu, and now you've got all my mates making fun of me. Thanks a lot!"

And with that, he walked off.

I've never seen Thomas angry before. It's weird, but it made me suddenly really, *really* fancy him. Which is a pity, as he obviously now hates me. Which is fair enough. I shouldn't have said anything to Hannah.

6:10 p.m.

I still feel terrible about upsetting Thomas Finch. I can't stop thinking about him. I've realized that if I feel this bad about being hated by someone I fancy, how bad must it be to be brokenhearted about someone you truly love?

Then I got to thinking about Mum. At some point it's going to be completely over with the Boy Toy and her heart is bound to get another dent in it.

I don't want that to keep happening. I don't want Mum to get hurt anymore. That's why she'd be better off not getting into relationships. She's better sticking with us, so we can look after her.

7:13 p.m.

I just met up with Hannah and Loops at Hannah's house and we split an enormous bar of chocolate. I couldn't enjoy it, so I just came home. I keep thinking about Mandy's broken heart and Mum possibly being hurt again and about Thomas Finch hating me. And I don't understand why, but my heart is feeling sore. I think I'll go to bed early.

I didn't think I cared about things so much.

Saturday, September 5

◎ LYING MODE ◎

All Grown-Ups are liars. There are two types of lies: White Lies and Filthy Dirty Lies. It's probably best not to be too hard on your Grown-Up or Grown-Ups if you catch them telling lies. After all, teenagers lie to Grown-Ups at least ninety percent of the time, so we should probably keep quiet and be grateful for everything they don't know about what we get up to.

My mum tells White Lies all the time, especially to Auntie Julie when she turns up at our house wearing clothes that don't suit her—like at the picnic. She only does it to save Auntie Julie's feelings.

But the other week she told Auntie Julie she wasn't feeling well and was going to have an early night—and then she suddenly felt better again and went out with the Boy Toy! Of course Auntie Julie found out—you can't keep a secret in Brindleton. That's a Filthy Dirty Lie, all right! I think Auntie Julie's still annoyed about it, though she hasn't confronted Mum.

I think Mum's been lying to herself recently, when she's been saying that it's just a bit of fun with Stuart. And—much more seriously—she's been lying to us when she said that no, she hasn't been staying out all night.

We *know* she's been lying, Mandy saw her creeping up the stairs one time. She called Mum a "dirty liar" right to her face—and Mum didn't even overheat! She just laughed.

Yet another reason I should be ringing ChildLine.

Mandy has reached new levels of Angry Mode, and the fact that the Boy Toy is back on the scene (and coming round on Saturdays) is only making it worse. Mandy's taking it out on everyone. She even called me the worst Filthy Dirty Liar in the world, due to a recent incident concerning her favorite nail polish.

Yesterday, we were at breakfast and I swore that I had *not* borrowed Mandy's nail polish and *not* forgotten to put the lid back on properly (which ruined it). Then I realized that I was *wearing the very nail polish*—I'd forgotten to take it off!!! I didn't know what to do, so I just kept denying it, even though Mandy was pointing at my hands, unable to speak for rage and shaking her head in disbelief.

But despite Mandy's anger-management issues, we are

somehow having a temporary truce while we work together to get rid of Stuart.

Mandy seems to be treating it as her life's mission. It's as if she's taken all her anger and disappointment about Joshua Weston and directed it at Stuart. Sometimes we talk about the Stuart problem at night before we go to sleep. We rack our brains to think up how we can annoy him and put Mum off him. In some ways, it's the best we've got along in ages.

Mandy called a third Council of War meeting with Jack and me last night.

"So the Boy Toy's got back in with Mum," she said, her brow furrowed, "which is his plan. His ultimate goal is moving in and taking over."

Mandy was pacing up and down the Cupboard (which is difficult; you have to do one step and then immediately turn and pace the other way). Jack and me were huddled in my bottom bunk.

"I think he's okay," said Jack, who still thinks Stuart's fantastic due to the piggy bank (which means, for anyone that's interested, that the price of Jack's lifelong approval is $7.99).

"Jack, do you know what will happen if Mum marries Stuart?" said Mandy. "Let me tell you. He won't take us to Disney. No, that's the *last* thing he has in mind for us. When he is in charge, we'll have to spend all day every day recycling and making compost. He'll probably make us *throw out the TV*. Tell me, Jack, is *that* what you want to happen?"

Jack looked scared.

"No," he said in a small voice.

I thought Mandy had laid it on too thick with this massive Filthy Dirty Lie, so I said, "It probably wouldn't be as bad as that, but we still don't want him ordering us around, do we?"

"So are we getting rid of him?" Jack asked.

Mandy gave an exasperated sigh. Obviously we *do* still want to be rid of him, but it would be dangerous to admit this to Jack, who'd announce it at the next family mealtime.

"We just want to be sure they're right for each other," she said, in Lying Mode, "and you can help us. You have to tell us anything that might be useful, anything you overhear or that Mum or Stuart tells you. Can you do that?"

"Yes," said Jack. "I'm a *brilliant* spy. I've got my spy kit, I'll use that."

10:45 a.m.

I got back from Hannah's to find Mandy waiting for me in the hall, wearing her T-shirt with the giant logo on it.

"Stuart's here! Go up and get into your T-shirt with the logo on it!" she hissed. "I've got Mum wearing hers."

I ran up and changed, then sauntered into the kitchen, where Stuart was happily drinking a cup of coffee as if it was his kitchen. He noticed my T-shirt but didn't say anything, just blinked a couple of times. Me, Mum and Mandy looked like a logo convention.

"Don't worry, Katie," he said, in Friendly Mode. "I'm not here to monopolize your mum, I just came round to see if Jack would like to go fishing! The stuff's in the car."

FRIENDLY MODE

This is not a bad mode for Grown-Ups to be in. It means they are doing their best to make you and other people like them...which makes your life a whole lot easier.

So there was Stuart, in full Friendly Mode. Yeah, right! In full Lying Mode, more like. As if he really wanted to spend time alone with Jack, the burping boy of Brindleton. It's so obvious he's just doing it to get in Mum's good books.

"You've got a *car*?" Jack pushed past Stuart and ran outside, where there was a little red vintage sports car, a

Triumph Spitfire with its top down and some fishing rods sticking out of the back. I couldn't believe it! Normally Stuart gets the bus. He's been keeping this from us. *More* lies! And how hypocritical—going on about the environment and secretly keeping a gas-guzzling sports car!

"Yes," said Stuart proudly, "meet my other girlfriend. Been off the road a few months, you know what these old cars are like. But now she's running like a dream."

Mum stood in the door of our house holding Rascal and looking worryingly impressed by Stuart's cool car.

"Can I go fishing, Mum?" Jack turned to Mum, his eyes shining. At this point Mandy made a *harrumph* noise and stomped into the house.

"Of course you can," said Mum, "just be back for lunch. I'll make something special—you'll be hungry with all that fresh air."

Stuart tried to look pleased at the thought. Lies upon lies upon lies!

"Now we can have a morning with just the girls!" started Mum, but at that moment Mandy reappeared in the hallway.

"I'm off to Lucy's house," she said, bad-temperedly pushing out of the door. "I'll be back at lunchtime."

"But, Mandy . . ."

It was too late. Mandy was gone.

"Looks like it's just the two of us," I said.

"Great," said Mum, in Friendly Mode, "how about painting our toenails?"

USEFUL HINT

If your Grown-Up is in Friendly Mode and wants to spend some time with you, humor them. The useful bonding experience should make them much easier to operate to your advantage.

12:30 p.m.

So we painted each other's toenails and agreed that it was a miracle Jack had agreed to do something that wasn't on the computer and was outdoors, and that he even looked like he might actually enjoy it.

Then Mum had to get serious. Ha! I *knew* she hadn't really wanted to spend quality time with me. After all, apart from when I was sick, she hardly ever does anymore. What a Filthy Dirty Lie!

"Katie, you may be wondering why Mandy's in such a bad mood," she said.

"I thought she was just being normal," I said. I mean, it's true. Grumpy and Angry Modes are Mandy's default settings these days.

Mum shook her head.

"It's because I told her that Stuart's going to stay over, just occasionally, on the sofa, of course. It's silly for him to go all that way home to Oxford only to come back on Sunday, isn't it?"

"I suppose so," I lied. I smiled at her and she looked relieved. But inside I was feeling a rising panic. I made my excuses and came upstairs to write this, in the hope I could get things clear in my head. This is not good at all.

And I've remembered Mum said you should only have sleepovers with someone you love. So does that mean she might love the Boy Toy? I don't think she can, but now that there's a danger of it, we have to act fast. Love Mode is the hardest one to switch a Grown-Up out of.

Saturday, September 5: 10:05 p.m.

☉ DISAPPOINTED MODE ☉

If your Grown-Up is in Disappointed Mode it's probably because you have let them down in an enormous way. This is the worst mode your Grown-Up can be in. It is even worse than Angry Mode because it can't be treated with the Avoidance Technique. The only way your Grown-Ups can be switched out of Disappointed Mode is if you do something, anything, that will make them proud of you.

I'm writing this on my bunk, with antiseptic cream all over my right cheek. Mandy and I are confined to the Cupboard—we're officially in *loads* of trouble with Mum. She is in Disappointed Mode, and nothing we do will be enough to snap her out of it . . . she may never be proud of us again. This could last for years!

After we painted our toenails and had our little talk, Mum was so relieved that I didn't kick up a fuss and so relaxed that—miracle of miracles—she forgot to cook, so when Jack and Stuart and Mandy got back we had beans on toast. Jack was on a high after the fishing trip and Stuart was making such an effort I almost felt sorry for him. (I must stop these thoughts, I have to focus on the fact that Stuart has evil motives for anything nice he does.)

"Do you like our new T-shirts?" asked Mandy innocently, over lunch.

"I'll be honest with you," said Stuart. "I don't see the point of paying extra to give some rich corporation free advertising."

"I don't know why Mandy spent so much money," said Mum. "We usually pay much less for our T-shirts, don't we, girls?"

Stuart looked concerned.

"When clothes are very cheap you have to make sure they're not made in sweatshops—" he started.

"Anyone for ice cream?" said Mum, in her overly bright voice.

"I'm not sure," said Mandy. "Are we *allowed* to eat ice cream, Stuart? Or is it made by exploited orphan Eskimo children out of polar bear fat?"

"Mandy!" warned Mum.

"It's okay," said Stuart, smiling. "She's funny."

This annoyed Mandy even more.

As the day progressed, I realized Mum and Stuart were making an effort to have sort of a "family weekend." Which included Saturday night together, with Stuart supposedly staying over on the sofa. It was an unlucky coincidence that Mandy and I were both around.

Usually when that happens, Mum takes the chance to go out, knowing she's got double babysitters for Jack, but in recent weeks she's obviously been thinking that we all need to "bond." Tonight she even suggested we *play a game*! How deluded can she be? In the end we all watched TV.

Mandy collared me in the kitchen about halfway through the evening.

"They're testing out how it would feel if we were a family, now that he's planning on staying over," she whispered. "So this is our chance. What can we do?"

I thought for a moment; then I had another flash of Evil Genius.

"Let's have a *fight*! You know, like when Mum says we've 'ruined the evening'?" I said.

Mandy's face lit up at the idea.

"Brilliant," she said. "I'll start it!"

We went back into the living room and sat down. Jack was on the sofa between Mum and Stuart (on orders from Mandy), so Mandy was in the armchair and I was cuddled up on the giant beanbag with Rascal—who was looking longingly at Stuart, as if he'd rather be cuddling him.

"You stole my eyeliner again," said Mandy casually.

"Did not!"

"Did too. Mu-um, Katie's always stealing my stuff."

I didn't like the way this was going. I'd agreed to have a fight, not have my good name and character called into question.

"That's not true."

"What about the nail polish, then?"

She had me there. I decided that the best means of defense was attack.

"It's not me who stole money from Mum's purse."

This was below the belt. It only happened once and Mandy was going to pay it back; the problem was that we don't live in the sort of house where there's enough money for some to go missing.

Mandy flushed bright red. I knew I shouldn't have brought that one up.

"Well, at least," she said, "I'm not writing a guide on how to operate Grown-Ups. How pathetic is that? Did you *know* Katie's doing that, Mum?"

Enraged, I looked over at Mum and Stuart. Mum looked like she was in Irritated Mode, whereas Stuart seemed to be trying to hide the fact that he was finding our conversation hilarious.

"You know what you are, Mandy?" I said, with as much dignity as I could summon. "You're a boring, moany old cow. No wonder Joshua Weston doesn't want to go out with you."

Suddenly Mandy was flying toward me, before I'd even finished the sentence! I felt her nails scrape painfully down the side of my face. I grabbed a handful of her hair and pulled as hard as I could. She had me pinned to the ground.

"Take it back!" she screamed.

"No, *you* take it back!" I screamed back.

Jack was dancing about in excitement.

"Fight! Fight!" he cried, his eyes shining.

Mum jumped to her feet and pulled us apart.

"*Stop it!* Go to your room, both of you!!"

As we slunk out of the room, I caught sight of Stuart, who no longer looked so amused.

When we got upstairs, I braced myself for an earful from Mandy, but she was disconcertingly cheerful.

"That was excellent!" she said. "Sorry about your face."

I looked in the mirror in the Cupboard to see three bright red scratches down my cheek. First the chin incident, then the giant sunburned nose and now this—yet another episode of freakdom sent by the gods to ruin my miserable existence.

"Thanks for poking into my stuff," I said, with some bitterness, as I rubbed antiseptic cream into my scratches.

"Well, you poked into mine, remember? And if you leave a notebook lying around for weeks, what do you expect? If you think writing 'Difficult Math Equations' on the front in black marker fools anyone, you are even stupider than I thought."

❗REMINDER TO SELF:

Keep guide under lock and key. Major breach of security.

10:32 p.m.

Something bizarre's just happened. Jack came bursting into our bedroom, wearing his night-vision goggles, all out of breath.

"You've *got to come*. I've been spying on Mum and Stuart—they're in the backyard—and they're talking about some sort of a *secret* Stuart has!"

We followed the very excited Jack to his bedroom, where he had the window open so you could hear what was going on down below. Mum and Stuart were having this urgent, hushed sort of a conversation.

". . . didn't think it was a big deal."

It was Stuart talking. Then there was a silence and then Mum spoke.

"Not a big deal? It's a *huge deal*. I can't believe you didn't think you could tell me. I was starting to wonder why you—"

"It's just that I've wanted to make a new start. I don't want people to know that about me straightaway; when they do, they don't see past it. I want people to get to know me for who I am, not what I was before. People put you in a box. It's been happening to me all my life."

"But we'll have to tell people sooner or later. You can't lie to my family about your past."

"Not yet, I'm not ready. I will tell them, but give me some time."

There was the sound of them kissing. We all made disgusted faces at each other. I hate that he could switch Mum out of Disappointed Mode so easily and then get her to kiss him. What's he got that we haven't?

"Let's go in," said Stuart.

When we heard the back door close, Mandy immediately hissed, "He's got a secret past!"

"What do you think it is?" I asked.

"He's been in prison; that must be it."

"But Gran Sutton got Uncle Pete's friend who's a police-man to check, remember? He's got no criminal record."

"What could it be, then?"

"He's an assassin?" suggested Jack hopefully.

"Maybe he used to be a woman or he wears women's clothes," said Mandy.

"That would be a good one," I said, "but his eyebrows are too bushy. Men who dress up as women usually have very neat eyebrows."

"Oh my God!" Mandy cried. "He could have a *disease*. Something horrible."

"Like the plague?" Jack chipped in. "Or scurvy?"

"He could have some embarrassing illness," I wondered aloud, "or maybe he used to *be* something, something that he's not anymore. Something terrible. Maybe he was a traffic cop!"

"I think it's something shameful for sure." Mandy looked excited. "This is *brilliant*! This could be the ammunition we need! We must find out what it is."

I don't think I'll get one wink of sleep tonight. Stuart doesn't want to be put in a box. But what box is it? We've got to find out.

It must be something pretty major, to distract Mum out of Disappointed Mode so easily.

Sunday, September 6

◎ ENERGY SAVING ◎

Energy is probably a big issue with your Grown-Up. If your Grown-Up spends too much energy on things that are not directly for your benefit or happiness, you are obviously being hideously and massively deprived. For optimum performance, ensure that your Grown-Up's energy is used to your best advantage.

For example, if you take your Grown-Up shopping and they show signs of fatigue, make sure you stop immediately and refuel them with caffeine and sugar-based treats. This should restore their energy levels. However, if your Grown-Up runs out of energy at home, in the evening, on the sofa—do not attempt to recharge them. Let them fall asleep. That way you can get the remote control.

It was odd, Stuart being around at breakfast today, sitting at our kitchen table in his bathrobe, looking far too much at home. I wonder if he's actually stayed on the sofa bed all night. Actually, I don't want to think about the alternative—it's too horrific.

Today is the last day of the school holidays, so Mum left the Boy Toy relaxing with the Sunday papers and took us to this giant outlet mall with a massive supermarket in it so we could stock up on school uniforms, pencil cases and all that stuff.

I'm always careful to monitor Mum's energy levels when we're shopping—today she was showing signs of extreme tiredness, so we took her for a coffee and a muffin to make sure she was "fueled up" enough to complete the trip.

The reason she was tired was because she had stayed up so late with Stuart last night, talking about his Big Secret. This was *not* a good use of her energy.

When we got back, Mum sent me down to the minimart, because despite being in the biggest giant monster supermarket I've ever seen in my life, she somehow managed to forget to buy bread. If she hadn't wasted all her energy, she would have been more alert and on-the-ball today. It's lucky we're old enough to know which uniforms we need; there was no way Mum was going to remember.

Nan was outside smoking again. She was wearing her pastel blue raincoat with the hood up.

"It's a hard life, being a smoker," she complained. "We're a dying breed."

Her cigarette packet said something along the lines of SMOKING KILLS. YOU WILL DIE A HORRIBLE, SLOW, PAINFUL AND UN-DIGNIFIED DEATH, YOU *TOTAL LOSER*.

"How's things?" I asked her.

"Oh, can't complain," she said. "'Hope for the best, expect the worst,' as they say. So, you're back to school tomorrow, then?"

"Afraid so," I said. "Back to loads of homework."

"Well, school's not the be-all and end-all." Nan stubbed out her cigarette against the wall. "I never paid a blind bit of attention myself.

"Better get back in. By the way, you can tell your mum this: the whole of Brindleton knows about her new man staying over."

I went in and got the bread. I was hanging about looking at the magazines, trying to read a couple of articles for free, when I heard Loops's unmistakable flirty laugh. It is an annoying, tinkling laugh that she reserves for boys she fancies.

I walked in the direction of the laugh, peeked round the corner and saw her in the Medicines and Diapers aisle. With Thomas Finch! They didn't notice me. They were too deep in conversation. Yes, Thomas Finch **CAN ACTUALLY TALK,** when he can be bothered. He just can't be bothered to talk to *me*.

Loops gave another of her tinkling laughs. Ugh. I felt incredibly annoyed. Then I felt annoyed at myself for being annoyed. Then I decided that I was really annoyed about the fact that it was raining. As I left the shop I said aloud, "Stupid rain!"

"It's probably not rain." Jonathan Elliott was lurking outside the minimart. I suppressed the urge to slap him very hard. (Now I wish I had.) He started walking along beside me. I quickened my pace. He quickened his.

"I would say that it's technically drizzle," he continued pompously. "That is when the drops have a diameter of less than half a millimeter."

"How fascinating," I lied. I was now speed walking at my top pace. Unfortunately, Jonathan Elliott's legs could more than keep up.

"I'm glad I bumped into you," he said. "I was wondering if you'd like to hang out with me . . . sort of go out?"

I slowed down.

"You're asking me out?" I said in surprise.

"I s'pose so," he replied matter-of-factly.

Now, at this point I should have just said, "No, Jonathan, I don't fancy you and I think you are a big know-it-all." I wish I had.

But—stupidly—I didn't want to hurt his feelings, so I said, "Sorry. I don't want to go out with anyone at the moment. I'm going to concentrate on my studies. It's not *you,* it's *me!*"

"That's cool," said Jonathan, nowhere near as devastated as I thought he'd be. "I prefer Loops. And, to be completely honest, Hannah would be my second choice. I only asked you because it looks like they're going to be going out with Thomas and Neil . . . so you're the only one who's free right now."

"I'm so flattered," I said sarcastically. "I am lost for words."

"By the way," Jonathan said, "what happened to your *face?*"

He was staring at the marks from where Mandy scratched me. I stomped off without even replying. I mean, really!

On the way home, I brooded about being Jonathan's third choice and decided that he was probably right, as there's nothing great or special or wonderful about me. Oh my God! I've got absolutely *nothing* going for me whatsoever!

Hannah is really good at acting; she gets big parts in all the school productions. Partly it's due to her being so pretty, but it's also because she doesn't just say the lines, she actually makes it seem real.

Loops is, of course, excellent at gymnastics. She can do a somersault in the air from standing, and you should see her on the beam. We went to see her in a competition and we were amazed at how fantastic she is.

And Mandy's been having piano lessons since she was nine, ever since a teacher told Mum she had real musical talent. She practices every morning for half an hour before breakfast on the keyboard with her headphones on. I don't know how good she is since I can't hear her because of the headphones, and she refuses to perform at school, but she must be at least half decent after all these lessons.

Everybody seems to have some talent for something, except me. I'm average at school, except at English, and even there I'm not exactly winning prizes—possibly because I'm a bit on the lazy side, to be honest.

I kidded myself that I was a world expert on the behavior of Grown-Ups, but the more I write this guide, the more I realize how much I don't know. Just look at how out-of-control Mum is! I'm only carrying on with it because Dad always told us that if you start something you should try to see it through till the end. "Nobody likes a quitter," he said, which is presumably why Nan Williams won't quit smoking.

I'm not even pretty, with my too-black hair and my flat chest and my legs that are knobbly-kneed and skinny. Hannah and Loops are getting curvy, but I still look like a boy.

Or a witch. Actually, more accurately, I'd call myself a flat-chested, pointy-chinned, knobbly-kneed witch-boy! Now that I think about it, I'm surprised Jonathan asked me out at all, even as a third choice.

So this was what I was thinking as I stomped home, making myself more and more annoyed at how much it stinks to be Katie Sutton.

Then I thought, *At least I can talk to Mum about this. After all, she must have had things like this happen to her when she was young. She'll understand.*

I hurried into the house and rushed through to the kitchen, ready to spill it all out. I really needed to talk to Mum. But of course, I'd forgotten that Stuart was still there and would probably be hanging around all day.

"So you're still here," I couldn't help blurting out.

"Katie, don't be so rude," said Mum. "Stuart likes to spend time with us. I don't see what the problem is."

"That's exactly the problem!" I shouted, and stomped up to my room.

No wonder Mum's so exhausted and absentminded. She's only got energy for Stuart these days.

Sunday, September 13

REMOTE CONTROL OPTIONS

You will be pleased to know that you can continue to operate your Grown-Up even when they are not in your immediate vicinity. Mobile phone, email and texting are excellent ways of remotely controlling your Grown-Up.

However, having a Grown-Up who is totally up-to-date can be a problem. For example, if your Grown-Up knows anything about computers, you can guarantee they will snoop on what you are up to online.

Worse than that, some of them might get their own social networking page—which has an Embarrassment Factor that's practically off the charts. Your Grown-Up advertising how desperate their pathetic life is, for the whole world to see . . . Horrifically tragic.

I've just had to text my own mother to find out where she is. This is the third time this week I've had to check on her whereabouts. So what's wrong with this picture??

When she first got a mobile, it took Mum ages to come to grips with it, but once she did she was always texting to see what I was up to. Most of her texts said, "Where r u? When u home?" Still, it was good to know she cared. She's definitely texting less recently because she's so busy being in Smitten Mode with the Boy Toy.

And it was the first week back at school! I can't help feeling a bit hurt she hasn't been around much and hasn't asked how things went. Especially as I've not exactly had a great week. . . .

The school bus, which takes us to our school in the town nearby, collects us at the edge of the village Park. So we all troop along at some stupidly early hour of the morning and stand there, even if it's pouring rain, waiting for the bus to pull up.

The older ones sit at the back. This is Ben Clayden, Harry and Jake and Joshua Weston. Also at the back are Shannon Gregg (boo) and her horrible friends, and Jenny Caulfield and her friend Sarah Jennings. Now that Jenny Caulfield and Joshua Weston are going out, Jenny still sits with Sarah, but Joshua hangs over the back of his seat to talk to her.

Mandy sits in the middle of the bus, doing everything she can to not look at Joshua and Jenny. She sits with her best friend, Lucy Parrish, and the rest of the Clones. Leanne

Gregg is also in the middle of the bus with some of her thug-like mates—we call them the Mutants. The Clones and the Mutants tolerate each other but don't mix.

This leaves Hannah, Loops and me sitting at the front of the bus with Neil Parkhouse and Thomas Finch and Jonathan Elliott and a few other year sevens, eights and nines from our and other villages. I don't mind, though. I like being at the front because then you get to get off first.

Looking good didn't used to matter so much when we were in elementary school, but suddenly there's this huge pressure to look brilliant *every single day*. I mean, we can't have Ben Clayden seeing us not at our absolute best. That's one excellent thing about being back at school—getting to see Ben Clayden every day.

One time last term, Hannah slept in and her hair was messy, so she looked awful. This boy in our year from another village who is called Matthew Hogg (you can guess his nickname) took a picture of her on his mobile and sent it to lots of other people. Hannah would now rather miss the bus than get on it with bed head, and so would I.

So I'd forgotten all about the pressure of the school bus, and having to get my hair right by about six in the morning, and remembering my stuff, and trying to not look any of the Mutants in the eye. It was okay on the first day, but on Wednesday I couldn't get it all together in time. Hannah had to go on without me, and I got to the bus stop just as the bus was pulling away. I could see Leanne laughing at me through the window. So I phoned home and asked Mum to drive me. She went into Irritated Mode because she had a class at nine and now she had to rush—but she still came and picked me up.

"Don't you *dare* make a habit of this," Mum said, clunking our decrepit car through the gears, "or I'll get Auntie Julie to take you next time."

She knows this is a good threat, as Auntie Julie is such a bad driver. Anyone who has to be her passenger gets out of the car at the end of the journey shaking uncontrollably.

So that was miserable. The only good bit about missing the bus and getting Mum to run me was knowing that my powers of remote control still work in an emergency.

Another low point was on Thursday morning when I had to present my summer project to the whole class. I was quite proud of it. I'd done it on Rascal and it consisted of a few pictures of Rascal together with some facts about him, like what dog food he likes and where his favorite walks are.

I was very unfairly picked on about it by Miss Mohair

Tights, who is actually called Miss Brown, but she gets the Mohair Tights name since she wears thick black tights and doesn't shave her legs, so the hairs stick through attractively.

"Really, Katie, this is the sort of presentation I would expect from a *nine*-year-old, not a thirteen-year-old. I'm extremely disappointed. I expected more from you."

The teacher's pet, Sophie Judd, smiled smugly, having got an A+ for her yawn-inducing "Art in Sixteenth-Century Italy" presentation.

At least lunch on Thursday was fun. Me and Hannah took our sandwiches up to the art department, which is always open, so we could spend the whole hour chatting and drawing while Ben Clayden worked on his latest art project—which is a weird sculpture made of bits of old wood. I don't really understand it, which proves it must be a work of immense genius.

Miss Hooper was tidying up the classroom and talking to Ben about what it's like to go to art school, so of course we were listening in. Miss Hooper is a bit eccentric, but she's all right and wants everybody to love art. She's even had her paintings in exhibitions.

"Sometimes we stayed in the studio all night, painting,"

she was saying to Ben. "Then we'd go and have breakfast in this little café round the corner."

I imagined myself going to art school and painting all night, but then looked down at my drawing of a bowl of fruit, which didn't look much like a bowl of fruit at all. Maybe not, I decided.

After school, me, Hannah and Loops went back to Loops's house and dyed our eyelashes with an eyelash dye kit. It didn't make any difference to mine seeing as they are dark anyway, but it made Loops's eyelashes look great. Because they're ginger, hers are invisible unless she wears mascara, which can look clumpy. So this eyelash dye worked excellently for her and for Hannah.

"We're stunning!" said Hannah, dancing round Loops's bedroom, massively batting her eyelashes.

"And now we'll look incredibly beautiful when we wake up! *And* when we're swimming!" said Loops.

"Well, I'm glad that your sad lives are now complete," I said, and Hannah threw a pillow at me, which of course started a massive and enjoyable pillow fight.

Friday was not so good. I wish I could use remote control options to summon a personal armed guard to defend me against evil Leanne.

As soon as we got off the bus, she and her sister Shannon cornered me on the playground and gave me a hard time. They threw my lunch box over the wall, spat on my backpack (which was totally gross of them) and pushed and jostled me.

This was revenge for the argument Mum had with Auntie Sarah in the supermarket. I'd been waiting for something to happen all week.

"That's for laughing at my mum," said Leanne as they strutted off.

Hannah came rushing over, too late, but at least the thought was there.

"Are you all right?" she asked, all concerned. I did feel shaken up, but I wasn't going to admit it.

"I'm fine, they're just idiots," I said.

"Well, I think you'd better come straight to my place after school," she said, "no arguments! Mum won't mind you coming early. You can text your mum."

So that's what I did. But the remote control function failed, due to Mum's phone having run out of battery (how was I supposed to know she was too busy rushing around after the Boy Toy to charge up her phone?).

The end result was a major row between Mum and Auntie Susan.

We were all sitting having lasagna and chips when the doorbell rang and it was Mum in Worried Mode.

"Thank God! Katie, I didn't know where you were! I was worried sick!"

So I explained I'd texted her and she explained her phone was out of charge and it would have been okay, but then Auntie Susan said, "Why were you so worried? Don't you think I'm capable of looking after your daughter?"

And then they had this huge argument. During which Auntie Susan suggested that perhaps Mum would have more idea what her kids were up to if she stayed at home more and that everybody could see she was spending too much time with her new man.

This caused Mum to instantly overheat and go into Angry Mode.

"I'll see you in the morning, Katie!" she said, before she slammed her way out of the house.

She really is turning into a different person.

Auntie Susan felt so sorry for me—what with me being a neglected child—she went into Doing Something Nice Mode and made us hot chocolate! Then we had popcorn and watched a movie and did our usual Friday-night lazing around and chatting.

There was only one annoying part, which was when we went to bed and Hannah chattered on yet again about Neil Parkhouse and Thomas Finch and Jonathan Elliott.

"I think Loops and Thomas look great together, don't you?" she said as we lay in our beds. "I think he likes her, especially now that her eyelashes look so great. He's just shy. Loops says she's going to ask him out if he doesn't ask her."

I pulled the duvet over my head, wishing I had a remote control and could turn the volume down on her prattling. I wish she would get a life and think about something else for a change.

What is it with everyone I love?

Thursday, September 24

◎ CONTROL LIMITATIONS ◎

Your Grown-Up is, unfortunately, a human being. They are constructed from flesh and blood, which means there are limitations on how much you can predict their perverse and annoying random behavior. If you had some sort of avatar Grown-Up you could right-click on them and choose the Eject option, or send them into some virtual orbit. But yours is real, so, sadly, these methods cannot be used.

I'd hate to have one of those robotic Grown-Ups, with the perfect house, who never have a hair out of place and when they're asked how everything is always say "marvelous." I've always loved the fact that Mum is normal and human and, just like most people on this planet, muddling on by. There's this saying, "Life is what happens when you're making other plans," which Mum has stuck on the fridge. It's so true. But even if life made Mum unpredictable at times, at least I knew where I stood. At the moment I just feel so confused.

I'm going to put my recent problems operating Mum

down to control limitations. I know it's a pathetic cop-out, but I haven't got anything else.

Still, only another day till the weekend. Although, Stuart becomes more and more established on our sofa every Saturday night (I wish he was some sort of avatar and I could eject him).

I'm going to phone Hannah in a minute, but thought I'd catch up on the guide first. I don't seem able to write as much in term-time as I did in the summer holidays, thanks to homework. Hannah has joined the drama group at school, like she threatened to. Fair enough, she did say she wants to be an actress, so the drama group is as good a place as any to start. And the teachers have been on at her to join for two years.

I'm being quite distant to let her know I'm fed up with her obsession with boys. Neil Parkhouse happens to be in the drama group. What a coincidence.

So on Wednesday lunchtimes Hannah is being all "dramatic" and pretending to be a tree with Ms. Edgerton and Neil Parkhouse and the rest of the suck-ups. Loops does gymnastics club, so I am alone.

This means that I have to spend the whole lunch hour hiding from Shannon and Leanne, who think it's a blood sport to hunt me down and torment me with various forms of torture, which include:

- pushing
- jostling
- tripping me (very original)
- taking my stuff and throwing it over walls or down stairs
- bra snapping (while saying "You don't need this!").

All they need is a bugle and a pack of hounds. Still, running around the school is keeping me fit.

To try to forget my troubles and because I was half thinking of confiding in her about the bullying, I went over to see Auntie Julie the other day. She was on yet another dating website, "surfing for love," as she puts it. Her house is becoming a real dump. I think she might be an Internet-dating addict. There were mugs everywhere half full of cold coffee, and plates with bits of takeout on them.

If she meets someone who isn't a lunatic and brings them back to her disgusting house, it's not going to do her any favors. What if Gary Barlow actually turns up? If he does I bet she'll wish she'd cleaned the toilet.

"Sorry about the mess," she said, not sounding at all

sorry. "Find yourself a space and I'll put the kettle on. I think I've got some biscuits somewhere."

I like it when she treats me the same as she'd treat my mum.

I managed to clear a space on the sofa and flicked through one of her celebrity magazines while the kettle boiled. Another soccer player has got married; there was a picture of him and his bride standing in front of a wedding cake that was three meters high.

"So what's going on, then?" Auntie Julie said, arriving with the tea and biscuits. "I feel like I've hardly seen your mum. I can't remember the last time we had one of our Friday nights!"

To cheer her up, I told her about Stuart and Mum talking in the backyard, repeating what we'd heard more or less word for word. She looked suitably impressed and interested.

"Now, *that's* a turnup!" she said, distracted from her bourbon biscuit for a second. "I should have guessed that there was something wrong with him. I mean, what kind of person doesn't take antihistamines?"

"So what do you think he's hiding?" I said.

"I can't decide. It may be a criminal past," Auntie Julie mused.

I felt better knowing Auntie Julie thought the same as Mandy and me. He is definitely *really sketchy,* that's for sure.

That's all I can think of to write for now. Off to phone Hannah.

9:27 p.m.

Oh. My. *God!!!!!!!!!!!!!!!*

Hannah is **OFFICIALLY** going out with Neil Parkhouse! But I can't believe she waited till I phoned to tell me. If I'd found out from anyone else I definitely would not be talking to her.

"*Please* don't be annoyed," she said. "I can't wait around for Ben Clayden forever."

"When did it happen?" I asked.

"Ten minutes ago! You know he's been texting me for weeks? This time he said in his text 'R U my girlfriend?' and I texted back 'Yes!' So it's definite."

"I don't suppose you can help yourself," I said, feeling pleased that I was the first to know about it. "You are obviously just *man mad.*"

"I wouldn't be surprised if Loops gets a text from Thomas Finch tonight," said Hannah.

"What makes you think he'd do that?" I said, too sharply.

"Because I sent Neil another text saying 'Thomas shld txt Loops 2 C if she is his.'"

"Hannah! Should you have done that?"

"Course I should, Loops is here now, it was *her idea*!" And then I heard this mad, hysterical laughing in the background. It was Loops. And there I was thinking that I was the first to know. What an idiot.

"Are you still coming for a sleepover tomorrow?" she asked.

"Yeah," I said, unenthusiastically. "S'pose so."

"Great, I'll make cheesy nachos."

Hannah's trying to be nice, but I feel cornered. It's like Hannah and Loops have our whole lives worked out. They've probably decided how many children we're all going to have. And I've a horrible feeling that in their master plan, I will be having lots of brainiac babies with slightly sticking-out ears.

Why is everything spiraling out of control?

Friday, September 25: 10:39 p.m.

I found it hard to get to sleep last night thinking about Hannah going out with Neil Parkhouse. I can't believe Loops and Hannah sent that text practically *ordering* Thomas Finch to ask Loops out!

Today, he was next to me in the lunch line. (On Fridays Mum lets us have a school lunch instead of a packed lunch, but it's nothing to get excited about; they've stopped doing fries, seeing as there are too many children who are over-weight or something.)

"What's up?" I said to Thomas in a friendly sort of a voice as I dolloped a huge splat of mashed potato onto my plate.

He just grunted. He's obviously still mad about the ro-mance novels thing. Then Loops came up, all hair-twirling and batting eyelashes.

"Hello, Thomas," she said, looking up at him adoringly, "mind if I push in?"

And he *let her*! Then the rest of the way up the line they were chatting away and I might as well have been invisible.

I am writing this at Hannah's house. Hannah's reading in bed. She wanted Loops to come along tonight too, but Loops had to go to her grandma and granddad's. At least that keeps her out of mischief, I suppose. I prefer the idea of her playing dominoes with her granddad to batting her eyelashes at Thomas, somehow.

As she'd promised, Hannah made me nachos and I let her babble on some more about Neil and Thomas. But it was a good evening. We talked about other things as well, and we watched a movie.

Before I went off to Hannah's bed, I made the mistake of telling Mum that everybody seemed to be pairing off and that I was not too happy about it. She went straight into Been There, Done That Mode (of course) and told me this long story about her and some friends and how exactly the same thing had happened to her.

⇨ BEEN THERE, DONE THAT MODE

This must be one of the most infuriating Modes that a Grown-Up can switch to. Whatever you do, they've done it before, and they insist on telling you all about it.

You can't win on this one.

I can't believe Mum! She's no better than the rest of them. It's maddening. The one time I've managed to get her alone to talk to her about my innermost feelings and she does that! I can't tell her *anything* anymore.

I had to act as if she was helping me, while thinking, *I don't* **WANT** *to hear about what you did back in the Dark Ages*. Why can't Grown-Ups just say, "I'm sorry to hear that, it must be rotten"? Why do they always have to relate it to their own distant youth, when nothing was like it is now?

She can't *possibly* understand.

11:30 p.m.

"Hannah," I said, a few minutes ago, "everything's not going to change, is it?"

"Of course not," she said. "You know what the magazines say: friends first. I won't let Neil Parkhouse or anyone else come between us, not ever."

I feel better about it all, now she's said that.

Saturday, September 26: 9:22 p.m.

It's now Saturday night and I can officially announce that I am the biggest idiot ever.

After the sleepover last night, Hannah and me went over to Loops's house. Loops was still in her pajamas when she answered the door with a triumphant look on her face. As soon as I saw her, I knew.

"Guess who got a text last night?" she said smugly.

Hannah jumped in the air and then hugged her.

"You got a text from Thomas? Let's see it!"

Loops showed it to us. It said "R U my girlfriend? If so C U at park 2morrow." He'd even done a smiley face.

"Oh my *God*!" shouted Hannah. "What are you going to *wear*?" They started discussing which stupid shirt Loops was going to put on to go to the park in.

"Are you okay?" I heard. I realized Hannah was talking to me. Her voice sounded quite far away.

"What? Yes, I'm fine."

Loops looked at me strangely.

"You *are* okay, aren't you, Katie?" she asked. "I mean,

you did dump him, after all, so you two are over."

She was absolutely right.

"Yeah, I'm like totally fine with it," I said. "I've just got a bit of a headache. I think I need to get home and lie down or something. You go on without me, I'll meet you later."

"Are you sure?" said Hannah, concerned.

"Yes, honestly, you two go ahead."

I don't know how I got home. I was in a daze. Even though I've had *weeks* to get used to the idea that Loops would probably get her mitts on Thomas, the reality hit me like a sledgehammer.

I've been kidding myself that I don't care, but the horrible truth can be denied no longer: I'm mad about him. And now—with my *full permission*—he is going out with one of my best friends. Well done, Katie, you've outdone yourself!

This is not like the way Hannah and me have been about Ben Clayden, just a silly crush. This is so different. I really, *really* like Thomas, but now I've messed everything up.

I sneaked up to the Cupboard and lay facedown on my bed for ages. There was no point talking to Mum, because she'd only go into Been There, Done That Mode yet again. After a while I crawled under the duvet. When Mum called me for lunch I said I wasn't hungry. How could I think about food?

I was thinking about Thomas. I thought about his brown eyes and his shy, lopsided smile. I thought about Loops and him having that long conversation in the minimart.

I'd like to say that I lay in misery for all those hours, but if truth be told, I did nod off for a while.

About midafternoon I heard the door to the Cupboard open, but I stayed under the duvet pretending nobody was there.

"Hey, you."

It was Mandy.

"Go away!" I said, trying not to sound sleepy, my voice muffled by the duvet. I felt the mattress sink a little as she sat down beside me. She actually patted me on the shoulder! For Mandy, that is a *huge* gesture, believe me.

"It gets easier," she said, in Sympathy Mode. I reckon she was thinking about Joshua Weston. Then she got up and left the room.

A little while later, Mum appeared. She sat stroking my hair for a while like she always does when I'm upset.

"Is it about everyone pairing off? Or is it more than that? Is it about a boy?" she asked.

I nodded, then whispered, "Don't tell Hannah and Loops or anyone. I don't want anyone to know."

"I won't tell anyone," she said, then added, "Katie, I know this might not help . . . but believe me, things that seem important when you're thirteen never stay that way. One day you'll look back and wonder why you cared so much. You might even laugh about it!"

I just *knew,* even before she started, that she'd go into Been There, Done That Mode. That's twice in one weekend! Grown-Ups are *so dense* sometimes. How could I *ever* in a million, billion, trillion, zillion years look back and laugh about this?

☹ SAD BUT TRUE FACT

Grown-Ups think that what happened when they were teenagers is not that different from what happens today. As if their sad and pathetic lives a hundred years ago could ever have anything in common with ours!

After Mum, my next visitor was Rascal, who jumped up, burrowed under the duvet and licked my face madly. I kept pushing him off, but he kept trying to get at me with his enormous wet tongue. I wondered if he was actually trying to snog me. That would be typical of my luck, if my first proper French kiss was from my dog.

Eventually I got up and washed my face. I found the strength to eat later on because (luckily) Stuart had got us all fish and chips and I could not resist, which shows that either I'm not *completely* devastated—or maybe I'm just a greedy pig who can stuff her sorry face no matter how bad she feels.

The only thing that made me feel a little better was Jack.

"I'm putting on a show," he announced after the fish and chips, "starring me."

Then he disappeared and in a few minutes reappeared wearing his Batman cloak and nothing else but a pair of red underpants. He bowed.

"Proud to present, the amazing Magico! Using my special power, I will now *read your minds*!"

"Okay," said Mum, "what am I thinking?"

Jack held his head dramatically, then said, "You are thinking that you need to give me double allowance for doing this amazing show!"

"Nice try," said Mum, laughing.

"What am I thinking?" said Stuart.

Jack made another big show of mind reading, closing his eyes in concentration.

"You are planning a journey. I see airline tickets. I see

Mickey Mouse. A trip to . . . Florida! You are taking us all to Disney World!"

Stuart looked at Mum and grinned.

"What's Katie thinking, then?" asked Mum.

Jack closed his eyes again.

"Katie is feeling sad," said Jack, "but she'll feel happy again if Mum buys her a new cell phone!"

He opened his eyes and gave me a big overexaggerated wink. Maybe he's right. If I can't have Thomas, a new cell would definitely help.

Tuesday, September 29: 8:59 p.m.

SOCIABLE MODE

When Grown-Ups are in Sociable Mode they smile and show their teeth and introduce each other to people and look delighted and interested in even the most boring situations. This function is called Making an Effort.

Some models of Grown-Up are more sociable than others. They're called "extroverts." They love being surrounded by people, chatting away. They are happy for people to pop in and see them any time—positively relishing surprise visitors.

Other models are "introverts," which means they prefer to stay home and do puzzles, jigsaws or crosswords, read books or watch TV—or all five activities at the same time.

Stuck home babysitting. **AGAIN.**

Mum is making an effort in getting to know more about Stuart's life and once again, leaving us! She's gone into Oxford for a drink with the Boy Toy and some of his friends—most of whom are teachers, like he is. I can't imagine a worse night out, spending it with a load of teachers. It would be my worst nightmare. Imagine a night out with our constantly angry math teacher, Mr. Catchpole, and Miss Mohair Tights. I'd rather go to the dentist to have all my teeth removed.

But now Mum and Stuart are a proper couple with what is known as a "shared social life," so they do everything together. How boring is that?!!

For a long time Mum was not in Sociable Mode at all. After Dad died she made no effort whatsoever. She couldn't bear to be among a crowd of people unless it was family, and even then she couldn't stand too much of them (which you can understand, seeing what our family's like).

So I should be pleased she's now enjoying going out and being sociable instead of staying in with us watching TV or having her usual Friday nights with Auntie Julie. I've made a resolution. I'm going to try to be pleased for Hannah and for Loops and everybody else. *That's* how mature I am.

I've given the Loops and Thomas situation some thought, and I've decided that if "going out" according to Thomas is the same as it was when he went out with me, then nothing is going to happen and I can deal with that.

Okay, so I like him. Far too much. But I'm not going to let that ruin my life. What is it they say about the birds of sadness? They may fly overhead, but you don't need to let them nest in your hair.

Feeling in Sociable Mode myself—and because I have nothing more exciting to do now that everybody is practically married—I popped in to see Great-Grandma Peters on my way home from school today. She was watching her favorite late-afternoon show on TV.

"This one's a sad case," she said, motioning for me to sit down. "She's about to have her home repossessed and she's desperate to win some money to pay off her debts. But greed will be her downfall, just like the rest of them."

We watched as the woman turned down sixteen thousand pounds.

"That's the best offer she'll get, I tell you," tutted Great-Grandma Peters, "but they *never know when to stop.* You're the first person I've seen all day. I've been sitting here all on my own!"

"I saw Nan in the shop," I said. "She said she saw you at lunchtime."

"For about five minutes! No, I'm all on my own here. Everybody's too busy to have any time for me. . . ."

At that moment, the doorbell rang. It was Auntie Susan, still in her nurse's uniform.

"Hello, Granny," she said. "Hello, Katie. So, what's going on?"

"She's going to get ten pence, I know it!" Great-Grandma Peters said hopefully, pointing at the TV. "She'll regret turning down that money! I've been saying to Katie that I've been alone *all day*."

I shook my head at Auntie Susan, who smiled and raised her eyebrows. An advert had come on the TV asking people to give money for dogs that'd been ill-treated.

"All Fido wanted was love, but instead he got kicked," said the advert. "Now he's wagging his tail again, thanks to Dog Shelter."

"That's a terrible thing, what people do to these poor dogs," tutted Great-Grandma Peters. "They should shoot the lot of them!"

"The dogs?" asked Auntie Susan, confused.

"No! The people who ill-treat them. Line them up and shoot them, *that's* what they should do. Along with the people who claim benefits when there's nothing wrong with them."

The doorbell rang again. It was Matthew, who wanted

some money from Auntie Susan so he could get sweets from the shop. Auntie Susan was having none of it. Immediately afterward Nan appeared, having finished her shift at the co-op.

"She thinks she's *neglected*," Auntie Susan whispered to Nan as Great-Grandma Peters ranted at the TV. The woman on TV had won seventy-five thousand pounds. The studio audience was screaming with excitement, whooping and shouting. The woman was crying; now she could pay off her massive debts and keep her house. You could see Great-Grandma Peters was bitterly disappointed.

"That was dumb luck," she said, "just *dumb luck*! There's far too many people here, I can hardly see the TV. Clear off, the lot of you!"

Wednesday, September 30

When I got home from school today, Stuart was there. Again. He's our regular surprise visitor these days. Only it's never a welcome surprise, not for me and Mandy, anyway.

He had been on some school trip to London and snuck off early to come and see Mum. Mandy was fuming in the kitchen.

"He thinks this is his home away from home," she hissed as she glugged down a can of Coke. "He *must be stopped*."

I wasn't sure. I was beginning to think that we might be interfering too much.

"Maybe we shouldn't give Stuart such a hard time."

"Yeah, and maybe he shouldn't be turning up on our doorstep without any warning!" Mandy said. "It's all part of his long-term goal to move in and take charge of our lives."

"I suppose you're right," I said. "I know, let's have bad table manners—you know, disgust him!"

"I reckon the food'll be enough," whispered Mandy, looking over at the pot of overcooked and slimy pasta mixed with kidney beans.

"Isn't it great that Stuart's staying for dinner?" said Mum, clearly in Sociable and Happy Mode as she glooped the pasta into five bowls. "What a nice surprise!"

Stuart smiled hopefully. Really, he doesn't get it. Talk about thick-skinned!

"Mmm, *pasta*!" I said enthusiastically. "I just can't eat enough of it!"

I started to shove a huge forkful into my mouth. I had to stop myself from gagging.

"Me too! I just love pasta!" said Mandy, doing the same.

"Was school okay?" asked Mum.

"Mnfughhhggggglmmmlshw!" I said, and a lump of congealed pasta dropped from my lower lip into my bowl.

"Glwgggrmmm mumphflggg!" added Mandy, then carried on eating, smacking her lips and opening her mouth too wide so we were all treated to the sight of her half-chewed pasta.

Stuart looked slightly revolted. It was bad enough having to eat the stuff without seeing it being showcased in Mandy's mouth in all its half-digested glory.

"Don't talk with your mouths full, girls," said Mum, shooting us a warning glare. She was beginning to switch from Sociable Mode to Irritated Mode.

"Sorry!" said Mandy, and then did an enormous, five-second-long sonic-boom sort of a burp. "Whoops! Sorry for that too!"

Jack looked at Mandy with awe and respect.

Then I pretended that my head was itchy. I scratched at my scalp furiously with both hands, right over my plate.

"There's head lice going around at school *again*," I lied, carrying on my exaggerated scratching act. I noticed that Stuart was slowly shifting his chair away from me.

"Katie!" cried Mandy, peering into my bowl and pretending to be shocked. "You've got head lice in your pasta! I can see them, they're *huge*! Some of them have got *wings*!"

"Not to worry," I said.

Then I took another enormous mouthful. Stuart looked like he might actually be sick.

At which point Jack unintentionally put the icing on the cake.

"Mum, I know it's banned at the dinner table," he said, "but I've done a *deadly* fart. It'll get over to you in a minute so you *might* want to hold your breath. It smells worse than one of Rascal's."

After Stuart left (straight after tea, unsurprisingly), Mum went into Angry Mode. I could tell she was working herself up to give us a serious lecture just by the way she stomped up the stairs.

"WHY are you being like this?" she shouted, appearing in the door of the Cupboard.

"Like what?" said Mandy innocently.

"You know what I'm talking about," said Mum. "You deliberately ruined things again! Why were you deliberately disgusting and antisocial? Can't you make more of an effort with Stuart? He's trying so hard."

"Sorry," I said quickly, even though I wasn't sorry, not one bit, "we were just being stupid. It was wrong of us."

She looked surprised.

"Well, at least you've apologized," she said, unsure of what to say next. Then she turned and went back downstairs.

TROUBLESHOOTING TIP

Saying "sorry" straight after you've done something wrong is a simple but remarkably effective strategy with Grown-Ups. Admit everything before their huge lecture and you can stop them in their tracks. For example, if they've been getting ready to have a five-minute foaming-at-the-mouth rant about how lazy and selfish you are, it's much harder for them to do it if you've just said, "I'm sorry. I am lazy and selfish, there's no denying it."

✺ INTERFERING MODE ◎

Some models of Grown-Ups just can't help themselves. They are born to switch to Interfering Mode at every opportunity. They think it's okay for them to meddle in other people's affairs. In fact, it is hardwired into their circuitry.

Last night, when I was getting ready to go to Hannah's, Mum asked how late me and Hannah stay up and what we eat. She wanted to know how much chocolate Auntie Susan lets us have and whether we are watching DVDs in Hannah's bedroom.

Mum has *never* asked these questions before! Maybe it's because Auntie Susan hinted she isn't taking enough interest in us since Stuart's been on the scene. Or maybe it's just Stuart's evil influence. He's obviously been saying things to her. She's been suggesting that we not go on the computer so much, and saying that we shouldn't rush our homework so we can watch TV but should spend a full hour on it. Which is *so harsh*!

Also, she thinks that as a family we should eat round

the table more instead of on our laps in front of the TV. Apparently it's better for our digestion. Though in my opinion, eating different food than what she cooks would be better for our digestion.

It's Stuart.

He's messing with our lives, just like we knew he would.

Honestly, Mum's becoming almost as bad as Nan—and Nan's the most interfering of all our relatives. Nan always thinks she has a better way of doing things, and she'll never tire of telling my poor mum and anyone else unfortunate enough to be within earshot her opinions. Which are often something along the lines of "Cut your coat according to your cloth" or "You can cross that bridge when you come to it." None of it ever makes sense, of course. Sometimes she even mixes them up and says stuff like "A stitch in time is worth a bird in the hand" and people actually agree with her!

She means well, but sometimes she does go too far—like when she took me, Jack and Mandy for haircuts not long after Dad died, *without consulting Mum*.

We did need haircuts, and obviously Mum had been too distracted to sort it out, but what upset her was that Nan got the hairdresser to give us all matching pudding-bowl haircuts, so we looked totally ridiculous.

This meant that not only did we have to cope with the fact that our dad had died, we also had to cope with looking like pudding-bowl-headed losers.

Gran Sutton used to interfere a lot when Mum and Dad were newly married, because they were so young. She would buy them things without asking if they were what Mum and Dad really wanted. One time she even ordered a carpet without asking what color they'd like(!). She chose a horrible mustard color, and Mum and Dad had to live with that carpet for years. They felt they couldn't complain because she'd paid for it.

I remember the day they saved up enough to get the mustard-colored carpet ripped up and put down laminate flooring. Mum was in Happy Mode like never before.

Speaking of Gran Sutton, we've not seen her for weeks. I know she's always been a bit annoying—but she's my *gran*. It feels bad that she's shut us all out like she has. That's the bad side of Interfering Mode, thinking that you know best and punishing people when they don't do things your way. It's really Controlling Mode.

None of this would have happened if it wasn't for Stuart.

1:16 p.m.

Friday-night sleepovers are now all about Hannah talking endlessly about Neil Parkhouse and Thomas Finch—she's getting as obsessed with boys as Mandy and the Clones! She keeps going on, practically in Interfering Mode, about how I should go out with Jonathan Elliott. She says that if I go out with him then we can all go out in a crowd.

I've said I'll think about it. I'm getting sick of staying in on my own on Saturday nights while Hannah and Loops go out on their so-called dates—which involve hanging about at the park. It's just what we've always done, but now it's with the boys.

I'm off to meet Hannah and Loops in ten minutes. My newly interfering mum has been quizzing me about where I'm going and when I'll be back. I could see her looking at my short skirt disapprovingly. She opened her mouth to say something but obviously thought better of it and shut it again. She knows I always get dressed up when we go to Oxford.

We're going to buy some bits and pieces for our Halloween costumes. Usually we trick-or-treat on Halloween, but this year we're old enough to go to Uncle Pete's annual party. The last few years Mandy and I've had to content ourselves with helping Mum get all dressed up for it, but now Uncle Pete's finally relented and said teenagers are welcome. Result! I know it's still a few weeks away, but we're ridiculously excited. Well, this *is* Brindleton, remember?

We're going to dress up as cats. It's an easy costume: black tights, leotards, cat ears and painted-on whiskers.

Stuart arrived ten minutes ago and he's gone straight off fishing with Jack. Jack loves it now, and he's got his own rod and fishing net. He looks happy—like a proper little fisherman. They go even if it's raining. Mum usually joins them for a picnic lunch—though I've noticed Stuart's started making his own sandwiches. "To save you the trouble," he says, in Lying Mode. To save himself tuna with cheese and brown sauce, more like.

5:00 p.m.

The trip to Oxford did not exactly go according to plan. Well, not my plan, anyway. And I did not expect to have one of the most embarrassing things to ever happen to me in my life happen this afternoon.

When I met Hannah and Loops at the bus stop, Neil Parkhouse, Thomas Finch and Jonathan Elliott were waiting too.

"What are *you* doing here?" I said rudely.

"We hear you're going to get your cat costumes," said Neil, "and we happen to be world experts on ears and whiskers, aren't we?"

"That's right." Thomas grinned. "And tails."

"I happen to know the best shop in Oxford for such things," said Jonathan. "It's near the covered market."

Hannah and Loops looked ecstatic that the boys were coming along, so I decided to remember my new mature outlook on life and not to spoil it by sulking—though I was tempted.

It turns out they're invited to the party at Uncle Pete's too, which isn't surprising, as half of Brindleton will be there.

"Did you know," said Jonathan, who had, of course, bagged the seat next to me on the bus, because the others were sitting in their cozy pairs, "that Halloween started as an ancient Celtic harvest festival? They thought the dead came back to visit the living on that night."

"Spooky!" said Loops, in her impressed voice. I wish she wouldn't encourage him.

The trip turned out to be fun. We watched some fantastic street performers, had a McDonald's (Coca-Cola was originally green—guess who informed us of that fact. . . .) and then we raided the party shop and got some cat stuff. Neil insisted on modeling a pair of cat ears on the way back to the bus stop, and Hannah giggled like it was the funniest thing she's ever seen in her tragic life.

"Did you know, if a cat falls off the seventh floor of a building it has a thirty percent less chance of surviving than if it falls off the twentieth floor?" said Jonathan.

"Shut up! I do NOT believe that," I said.

"Let's test it out," Thomas Finch said, winking at me. "Let's put the ears on Jonathan and chuck him off the top of something!"

I've got to admit, since he's been seeing Loops, Thomas has been more confident. He never used to speak up so much. And he's actually quite funny.

"Great idea," I said. I'm quite relieved he no longer seems to hate me. He seems to have forgotten the library incident. If I'm totally honest, my heart gave a little leap when he winked at me.

It was on the way back from Oxford that the radically embarrassing thing happened. Why is it always to me?

By the time we got on the bus there was room to stand. We all shuffled down the middle aisle.

I was holding on to the vertical bar thingy, swaying along like everyone else. Then, after a few minutes I heard the first snigger. Then there was another. I looked round, but I couldn't work out what on earth everyone was laughing at. I hoped it wasn't my legs, which I was worrying were looking skinny in my short skirt. Hannah and Neil were right at the back, so I couldn't see them, but I could tell by looking at Loops and Thomas and Jonathan that there was something funny happening.

"What?" I mouthed to Loops.

She just shook her head in despair and looked at the ground. Thomas and Jonathan were doing a sort of silent laugh. I looked round and saw that other people also seemed to be finding something funny and they were looking at *me*.

Next to me, sitting down, was an old gentleman. When I caught his eye, he looked pointedly down at his feet, where there was a carrier bag. I looked down at the carrier bag and saw that in it there was a broom, which he'd obviously bought at the shops. The broom had a long handle. It was then that the horrible truth became clear. Instead of holding on to the rail, I was actually *holding on to the broom handle*.

I leaped backwards, letting go of it as if it was on fire,

which is when the bus erupted in laughter. All the polite people who'd been smiling or quietly sniggering were now laughing out loud. I'd made their day.

"Didn't you wonder why it was *swaying*?" said Loops, when we got off the bus, my face still burning with shame, "And didn't you notice it was *bright red*?"

"Well, I can see it was an easy mistake to make," said Jonathan, which I thought was quite kind of him. Maybe he's not such a nerdy know-it-all.

"Don't worry, Katie," said Neil with a huge grin, "we know you can *handle* it!"

Now I'm hiding in my bedroom and may quite possibly never leave it again. Unless, of course, I take the next plane to the Himalayas. My donkey's waiting.

Saturday, October 3: 6:00 p.m.

I managed an hour in my bedroom reliving the nightmare of the bus incident; then I got bored and came downstairs. Auntie Julie's been on the phone. She had a date lined up for tonight, but she's canceled it after he sent her an email asking about the color of her underwear or something. Poor old Auntie Julie, *another* major pervert. As Mum's in Sociable Mode and going out on the town in Oxford with Stuart yet again, Auntie Julie wants to come and see us.

"Let's make it just the three of us girls . . . and Jack and Rascal," she said. "We'll have a pajama party!"

How sad is that? Wanting to have a pajama party at her advanced age. And calling herself a *girl*! Me and Hannah and Loops have pajama parties, and so does Mandy with Lucy Parrish and the Clones, but to have one with Auntie Julie just seems like a weird and wrong idea.

Still, she's very excited, so Mandy's canceled going to Lucy Parrish's and has gone down to the minimart to get pizza. I think Mandy sees this as a chance to ask Auntie Julie to help us get rid of Stuart. I'm not so sure. I mean, if

Auntie Julie was such an expert on things to do with men, she wouldn't be sitting in a living room full of empty take-out containers, on her own, drinking red wine and singing along to Take That, would she?

9:22 p.m.

It's official. Auntie Julie is both Fiendish *and* Cunning! We didn't even have to ask her help about Mum and Stuart—*she* brought up the subject. And she feels exactly the same way as us about the whole situation!

➥ FIENDISHLY CUNNING MODE

It has to be admitted, Grown-Ups can at times surprise you by being Fiendishly Cunning. This means that they "get one over on you."

For example, they might say to you that they don't think you're old enough to understand how the washing machine works. So you insist you can work it, and before you know where you are, you're responsible for doing your own laundry! This is Fiendishly Cunning Mode at work.

Auntie Julie arrived at our house not long after she'd rung . . . *in her pajamas and robe.* This is an example of the typically deranged behavior we expect from Auntie Julie. What if her car had broken down on the way?

I know it's only a few streets away, but still. . . . Stuart's obviously having an influence on me; I was thinking how environmentally irresponsible it was of her to drive less than a mile to our house.

Her pajamas were bright pink cotton with little pigs all over them, which would look cute on an eight-year-old, but didn't look *quite* so cute on Auntie Julie. They made her bum look even more epic than usual.

"Isn't this fun?" she said as we all sat in our pj's munching pepperoni pizza. Jack's pajamas had aliens on them, which did look cute.

It *was* fun, actually. We watched a movie that was suitable for Jack, then packed him off to bed—not without him protesting loudly, of course. After he brushed his teeth, I went into his room to tuck him in.

"Do you think Stuart will *ever* take us to Disney?" he asked.

"It's not looking likely," I said.

"Then maybe we should get Mum to marry a millionaire instead," he said, "and we could all live in a solid-gold house."

"That's a good idea," I said, imagining us all watching Mum snogging some random millionaire on a solid-gold sofa.

I went downstairs, where Auntie Julie had opened a bottle of wine—she let Mandy and me each have a sip.

"Children drink wine practically when they're *babies* in France," she said.

After she'd had a couple of glasses, she remarked—out of the blue, "Of course, they're all wrong for each other."

Mandy almost leaped off the sofa with excitement.

"You're **SO RIGHT!**" she said. "She's not *in love* with him. She's only with him because she's lonely and he turned up on her doorstep and isn't completely hideous-looking or a mass murderer, so she's grabbed him."

Auntie Julie nodded. "She's been too desperate," she agreed. "She could do much better. . . ."

"You're right!" I exclaimed, just as excited as Mandy to find that Auntie Julie agreed with us. "If she *does* want to go out with someone, maybe in about five or ten years, she should go out with someone who's a top professional, like a doctor, or someone rich, like a famous soccer player, or a millionaire businessman—not some boring PE teacher whose head swells up whenever he goes near grass clippings."

Auntie Julie glugged back some more wine, then sighed again.

"Yes, she's wasted on him," she said. "But then again, perhaps they're happy together?"

"He's *five years younger than her*," Mandy shouted, "*and he's obsessed with recycling and he's got a giant nose*. How can she be happy with someone like that?"

Auntie Julie looked thoughtful.

Then I told her about Stuart never going to see his poor old parents and how he must be hideously selfish.

"That's terrible," Auntie Julie said. "It must break their hearts!"

We all agreed then that Mum could do a hundred million times better than Stuart. We convinced ourselves that it was our duty, as the people who loved her, to make sure Mum didn't throw herself away on someone not worthy of her. And then we remembered about the fact that he has some sort of dodgy secret from his past and thought of new terrible things it could be.

I told Auntie Julie, slightly tearfully, that I missed having Mum around.

"I miss her too!" she said. "We never see each other anymore! She's always with him!"

Then she seemed to go into a trance, she was so deep in thought. Or perhaps it was the effects of the wine.

"Okay," said Auntie Julie finally, through a mouthful of cold pizza, "if we're going to get rid of him, how are we going to do it? What have you thought of so far?"

"Not recycling," said Mandy, "and we wore T-shirts with logos on them . . . and we had a big fight in front of him . . . and Katie mowed the lawn to give him hay fever—"

"*Not recycling?* Wearing T-shirts with *logos*? Do you really think that's enough to persuade Stuart to give up your mum? That's *pathetic*! If her cooking hasn't put him off, then it's going to take a lot more than not recycling and a couple of logos to send him packing."

"I know, we're rubbish," I admitted. "That's why we need your help. You know how men's minds work, you've been out with lots through those dating websites."

Auntie Julie looked flattered, in a "woman of the world" sort of way.

"Well," she said, "in a case like this, you have to be extremely cunning. You have to think about how Stuart ticks: What does he find unattractive? Would he mind if he found out that your mum was married to the love of her life and that he's just a substitute? That sort of thing."

"He once said he thought punk rockers look hideous," I remembered.

"Exactly!" said Auntie Julie. "That's exactly the kind of thing we can use."

Auntie Julie is a genius! All along, I've been trying to use my expertise to put Mum off Stuart, when really I should have focused on making *her* less attractive to *him*! It is so obvious!

Over the rest of the evening we came up with a Fiendish and Cunning Plan, a plan so fiendish and cunning that it is guaranteed to work. A plan that will send Stuart running for the hills as fast as his trainers, which were not made in a sweatshop, can carry him. Ha ha! No more PE teachers on our sofa!

"You're amazing, Auntie Julie," I said as we headed upstairs to bed.

"I know," she said, "but you're the ones who have to make it work. And nobody must know about this. Not even Hannah, Katie. My life won't be worth living if this gets out."

Saturday, October 17: 9:00 p.m.

Nothing exciting has happened at school the last couple of weeks. I think I must be fed up or something, because I've not even had the heart to write this guide. Miss Hooper is entering Ben Clayden's sculpture in some art competition, as she thinks he's a genius. Which he is, of course. And Miss Mohair Tights's leg hair is getting seriously out of control— I swear it's *over a centimeter long*. Maybe she doesn't have central heating and uses it as some sort of leg insulation.

Hannah and Loops giggle away with Neil and Thomas on the playground, while Jonathan follows me around telling me that an ostrich's eye is bigger than its brain, or that porcupines float in water. It's actually been quite useful having Jonathan shadowing me—it means I'm not a total loser. But now and again, for example when he's telling me that a snail can sleep for three years, I'd almost prefer to be alone.

It's definitely getting colder, so Mum's making me wear my horrible shiny black coat that looks like a giant sleeping bag. I don't mind too much because Loops and Hannah both have identical horrible coats.

Last night at our sleepover, Hannah managed ten minutes and thirty-eight seconds without talking about Neil Parkhouse. I timed her. Not that I'm getting bitter or anything. Anyway, she talked me into going out with her, Loops, Neil, Thomas and Jonathan by bribing me with chocolate.

So this afternoon we all went—just for a change—to the park. Neil, Thomas and Jonathan kicked a soccer ball around while Hannah and Loops flicked their hair. Well, Hannah flicked her hair and Loops sort of twirled hers.

Then Hannah and Loops giggled a lot and flicked and twirled their hair some more while talking to Neil and Thomas, while I was left with Jonathan . . . again.

"Did you know that every time you lick a stamp, you consume a tenth of a calorie?" he said.

"Really?" I made a mental note not to help Mum with the Christmas cards this year, as I watched Loops look up at Thomas through her dyed eyelashes. I've seen her practice that look in the mirror.

I got this little ache of regret in my stomach, seeing them together. I've got to get over this.

"Guess how long a giraffe's tongue is," said Jonathan.

"I dunno," I said.

"Fifty-three centimeters! They can clean their ears out with them."

I wondered if Jonathan could clean *his* ears with his tongue, him being such an expert at using it. I nearly laughed out loud.

At that exact moment, he lunged! I think he was going to try to kiss me, but he didn't get that far. As soon as I saw his face loom up, I dodged him. I was still thinking of him as having a fifty-three-centimeter tongue.

"I've got to go," I squeaked, then I ran most of the way home. While I was running I was thinking what guts Jonathan has to try something again after letting me know that he prefers Loops and Hannah to me. Does he think I have no pride?

I felt like the biggest and stupidest reject third wheel in the history of reject third wheels.

As if that wasn't bad enough, when I got home Mum and Stuart were, of course, snuggled up on the sofa.

"Are you all right?" said Mum, looking hideously happy.

"Fine," I lied, and came up here to write this.

If Mum wasn't with Stuart, I could have told her what happened. She'd have made me a cup of tea and gone into Been There, Done That Mode and we'd have had a laugh about it.

Aren't Grown-Ups supposed to put you first and notice when you're not happy? Isn't that what they're meant to do? Mum used to notice, till Stuart came along. Her Intuitive Function has obviously shut down due to the fact that she *no longer cares.*

INTUITIVE FUNCTION

Intuitive Function can be a good thing in a Grown-Up, because it means that they are sensitive to when there is something wrong and care enough to notice. However, the downside is that if your Grown-Up has good Intuitive Functions, they can often switch to Suspicious Mode—especially when you are up to something. This can be most infuriating. The only way to stop it is to distract them at the exact moment that their Intuitive Functions might start to kick in by saying something like "What's that noise?" or "Can you smell grapefruit?" This is called the Distraction Technique.

So now I'm sitting here in my bottom bunk in the dark, using my stupid headlamp from stupid Stuart so I can write this. Rascal has just come to find me. He always knows when I'm fed up. He's licking my face right now, so I can't write any more.

Saturday, October 17: 10:30 p.m.

MEMORY CAPACITY IN YOUR GROWN-UP

Grown-Ups' memory capacity usually reduces as they get older. For example, a middle-aged Grown-Up will forget things like where they put the car keys, what they've done with their mobile phone and the fact that they promised to pick you up from an after-school club.

However they will *always* remember how many days you're grounded for and—when you're out together in public and they're stuck for conversation with strangers—every single, embarrassing detail of your potty training.

Much-older models of Grown-Ups will forget your name and will usually call you the name of every relative you have and the dog before they get to yours. They will also quite regularly put milk in the washing machine, the newspaper in the fridge and their dirty socks in the magazine rack.

I'd been in the Cupboard, cuddling Rascal and listening to music, when Mandy came in after having had a row with Lucy Parrish about something. We had a moan about how rubbish our friends are and how we can't even watch TV in our own house without having to put up with Mum and Stuart canoodling on the sofa.

"I don't know how they manage to kiss with his big nose getting in the way," I said. "They must have to do some sort of sideways maneuver."

"It's an outrage," said Mandy, picking purple nail polish off her toenails. "Mum's so absentminded thanks to the Boy Toy. She's forgotten to pay half the bills. We've had three red reminder letters. And you've got to admit, she's not on top of basic stuff like money for school or even our pocket money. At least it's only two weeks till the Cunning Plan."

"They'll probably have got married by then," I said, "*and* she'll be pregnant with triplets. They'll probably move out of the house and forget to tell us where they've gone."

Sunday, October 18: 3:27 p.m.

Mum has clearly not just forgotten to pay a few bills . . . her memory capacity has been so compromised by being in Smitten Mode that she's forgotten we exist! She certainly isn't taking our feelings into account anymore.

It is hideous to have to write this. It makes me feel so sick to my stomach. Okay, here it is.

Stuart isn't on the sofa anymore. This morning I bumped into him coming out of Mum's room wearing his boxer shorts—which I noticed had hearts all over them. He didn't even have the decency to look ashamed! He just gave me a cheery smile!

I pretended to be cool about it, but I had to go and sit down on my bed because my heart was beating so fast. I couldn't write about it till now . . . I was trying to pretend that it wasn't true. But I've got to admit it, the horrific fact is this: they are sharing a bed. The bed Mum used to sleep in with Dad. How *could* she? Has she forgotten all about Dad already?

At breakfast, they were discussing going on a mini-break again. It was hard to swallow my Wheaties while having to hear about the different cities they could go to for their weekend getaway.

"Prague is supposed to be stunning," said Stuart, munching his toast and jam.

"Venice is romantic," sighed Mum. You'd think she'd been there, the way she talks. I think she's been to France on a school trip and that's about it as far as foreign travel is concerned.

Stuart's done interrailing round Europe and he's been to India, which I have to admit is quite impressive. I suppose that's the sort of thing you can do when you don't have kids at too young an age like Mum and Dad did.

"What about Paris?" suggested Jack. "First we can see the Eiffel Tower, then we can go to Notre Dame and *then* we can go to Disneyland Paris—it'll be so cool!"

You've got to admire his optimism. I don't have the heart to tell him that people who're going on a mini-break *don't* want to be followed around by an eight-year-old boy. No matter how good he is at burping the theme tune to *Star Wars*.

I made a great show of not putting an empty cornflakes packet in the recycling. Then Mandy cleared her throat loudly and put tea bags in the normal trash bin instead of in the compost bucket. Mum and Stuart didn't even notice; they were obviously in Delirious Mode thinking about croissants and complimentary bathrobes. We are Officially Invisible!

3:27 p.m.

Hannah and Loops just turned up, wondering why I ran off last night. I told them about Jonathan lunging at me. Hannah laughed hysterically, but I noticed Loops was quieter.

"Don't you like him?" said Loops.

"No. And even if I did, he's made it clear that he's only interested because you and Hannah are not available."

"Really . . . ?" said Loops, looking pleased.

"So *how* long did he say a giraffe's tongue is?" asked Hannah, and she dissolved into laughter again. Soon she and Loops were practically holding on to each other in order to stay standing up.

"Well, I'm glad I'm providing you with entertainment!" I said, slightly hurt.

Hannah wiped the tears from her eyes. "Oh, sorry, but it's *so funny!*"

I decided to ignore their incredible childishness.

I wasn't sure I wanted to know, but I couldn't stop myself from asking. (Maybe I'm a glutton for punishment.) "So what happened after I left?"

"Nothing much," said Loops.

"Come on!"

"Well, Neil kissed me . . . but not in a serious kissing way," confessed Hannah, dreamily. "He's so . . . !" She was lost for words. That's love for you.

"What about you and Thomas?" I asked Loops as casually as I could.

"We just talked," she said.

I felt relieved. But who am I kidding??? Loops is not one to take no for an answer. It won't be long till she's got him where she wants him (in the teenagers' shelter).

I've *got* to stop feeling this way about Thomas Finch. It means I've got a secret from Hannah and Loops, and I've **NEVER** kept anything from them before.

Friday, October 23: Midnight

◎ SAD MODE ◎

When a Grown-Up goes into Sad Mode, it is usually because of something that has happened. It could be something trivial or it could be something much bigger and more important. You might not even be able to work out what it is. There are lots of clever things you can try, like mode-switching and the Distraction Technique or a great big soppy cuddle . . . but sometimes you have to accept there's not much you can do except just be there and try not to make things worse.

Today was the anniversary of the day Dad died. It's always a difficult day. I'm glad that out of respect Mum didn't ask Stuart over. She was very quiet at breakfast and when we got home from school. She's in Sad Mode.

I know all about Sad Mode in Grown-Ups; it could be my specialist subject. After all, I saw Mum go through the whole process.

It was like losing two parents—Dad and the happy mum we had before he died. That's why it was so difficult and mixed up. We wanted our happy mum back, but she had disappeared. She tried to hide that she was in Sad Mode, but it was there even when on the surface we were having fun. It was hiding behind her eyes.

The good news is that things usually improve, if Grown-Ups get the right support. It may take a while, but things do get better.

That's life. Nobody can be happy all the time; every Grown-Up gets sad at some time in their lives. Don't take it personally. I used to with Mum. I'd think, *If I was not so horrible and selfish, then she would not be like this,* or, *We're not important enough for her to snap out of it.* She couldn't help it; she needed time to get over it and, eventually, she did.

But the anniversary still gets her. In a funny way, I'm glad about that. It shows that Stuart hasn't completely replaced Dad. It shows that despite the Memory Capacity issues, she hasn't forgotten him. And she never will, I should have realized that. She'll always be in Love Mode with him.

I'm using my headlamp to write this again. I have to admit, it has come in handy for this guide, if nothing else. I'm at Hannah's, and she's just gone to sleep. This week Jonathan Elliott didn't come near me. Even though he might be the most stubborn person I know, even *he* got the hint last weekend.

I almost miss his constant presence, him telling me that there's no word in the English language that rhymes with month, orange, silver or purple, or that a group of twelve or more cows is known as a "flink."

Yesterday was horrible. I spotted Thomas and Loops *holding hands* on the playground. Seeing it actually made me feel awful. He pulled his hand away when I walked up, which made me wonder if it was more to do with her than him.

But on a brighter note, Mr. Catchpole has taken a leave of absence because of stress and has been replaced with Miss Allen, who all the boys fancy because she's twenty-four and wears tight jumpers. And other good stuff has happened.

The highlights of this week were as follows:

1) Mum has a cold, so she hasn't been cooking and we've had decent food.

2) Mum backdated all the pocket money she forgot to give us, so we're rich.

3) When I went over to Great-Grandma Peters's house she gave me five pounds for cleaning her kitchen. Now I'm even richer.

4) Me and Hannah and Loops have had a running joke about giraffes' tongues all week and even now I am snickering.

Saturday, October 24: 1:00 a.m.

Why can't I get to sleep? Too much to think about, I suppose. Tonight Hannah was incredibly sappy about Neil Parkhouse. He's *so* funny. He's *so* good-looking. He's *so* good at soccer. The usual. I decided to ask her the big question.

"So are you in love?"

Hannah wouldn't give me a definite answer, so I guess she is. Then she dropped the bombshell.

"I got permission from Mum, and me and Neil are allowed to go up to Oxford to the movies next Friday night, as long as his mum drives us home. . . ."

Her words trailed off as she saw the expression on my face. Friday night has always been our sleepover night for as long as I can remember. I can hardly remember *ever* not spending Friday night at Hannah's house.

"Oh . . . look . . . I'm sorry," she said. "I had to say no to Saturday because of Uncle Pete and Auntie Paula's party, so I didn't want to say no to Friday as well in case he thought I was putting him off. Look, I'll text him right now and cancel it."

"It's all right," I said. "I mean, this was going to happen someday, wasn't it? It could have been me. You go out. I'll be fine."

Hannah gave me a huge hug.

"You're my best friend and double cousin in the world," she said.

I smiled. But inside I was feeling sad. It was like something was ending, and I know that feeling well.

1:20 a.m.

It's time to tell you about Dad's last day. If sadness is about endings, this was his.

Mandy and me took turns sitting with Mum beside Dad's bed while the other one walked around the grounds with Sheila from the local child bereavement service.

Sheila started seeing us in the last few weeks of Dad's life, and she was very matter-of-fact and easy to talk to. She explained things we didn't understand and we could talk about anything at all, including things that we were worried or unsure about. She wore a blue fleece that was exactly the same color as her eyes. It's funny the things you remember about a person.

People like Sheila should get giant, enormous medals.

You don't know they're out there quietly doing jobs like that until something happens to you, and then . . . well, you're just glad they're there.

Uncle Dave came by at lunchtime and had some time with Dad. When he left he couldn't speak to us, he just hugged us and left. Gran and Grandpa Sutton had come the night before and stayed most of the night, and they were going to come in again that night to give Mum a break.

I went in and saw Dad late that afternoon. Mum was holding his hand, and he was going to sleep, then waking up for a bit, then going to sleep again.

One of the times he was awake, he looked straight at me. It was as if he was trying to memorize my face; he just looked and looked. Then he whispered something, but I couldn't hear, so I moved closer.

"Are you fantastic?"

I had such a big lump in my throat I could hardly reply.

"Yes."

"Are you brave?"

"Yes."

"Are you a porcupine?"

I shook my head and I was biting my lip so I wouldn't cry in front of him.

He just smiled this lovely smile and closed his eyes again.

So those were my dad's last ever words to me: "Are you a porcupine?" Try explaining *that* to people.

Auntie Julie took Mandy and me home, or rather to Auntie Susan and Uncle Dave's house, where Jack was.

On the way I was looking out of the car window at the sunset, thinking that you never know when it's gone, you just know that one moment it's there and then somehow it isn't anymore. Like Dad. Sunsets are so *quiet*.

Sheila kept visiting us for quite a while after Dad died. One time I told her about what I'd been thinking about on our way home that night, about the sunset, and she said *the best thing ever*. She said, "You know what I think whenever I see a sunset? I think that when the sun has gone and we can't see it anymore, it's just arriving somewhere else."

Maybe that's how we need to think of all endings, like the ending with Hannah and our Friday-night sleepovers. An ending is usually also a beginning. It's just we're never quite sure what it's the beginning of.

2:00 a.m.

I've just read over everything I've written tonight. I wrote about how Mum was in Sad Mode for so long and how I wanted to get the old happy Mum back.

I don't suppose I quite know when it happened, it must have happened gradually, but the truth is, she's back. Our happy mum, the one we missed. Apart from today, which is understandable, Mum's not in Sad Mode anymore. And I haven't wanted to admit this, but the truth is *I think Stuart has a lot to do with it.*

So what's going to happen after we do the Cunning Plan? What will happen then?

Friday, October 30: 4:27 p.m.

⊚ WISE MODE ⊚

Very occasionally, Grown-Ups will switch into Wise Mode. This is where they actually speak a great deal of sense and say something filled with great insight and perception. This is a very unusual occurrence. Do not expect it to happen very often.

I said before that when my dad died Love Mode was the last mode that he lost, because it was the most important one.

But before that, Dad was in Wise Mode. I suppose he wanted to make sure he told me everything he thought I'd need to know. He said something to me when he was ill that I've never forgotten.

He said, "I've spent my life thinking things were important that aren't. Things like the size of your house or the type of car you have or where you can afford to take your family on holiday.

"I thought I was right to want the best for you all. But you know what? None of that matters. All that matters is that people love each other. Love your family and your friends and treat people right. Nothing else is important."

I often think about what he said, when I wish that we lived in a bigger house or that we could go on holidays abroad like other people do.

I'd love to live somewhere more exciting than Brindleton, like London. But if Dad's right and nothing matters except relationships and your family, then it would be pretty idiotic to go and live someplace where I don't know anybody. Unless I got lots of new friends—better-looking and more interesting ones than my relatives (which would not be difficult). But something makes me think that's not *quite* what my dad had in mind.

Family is SO important in Brindleton. Perhaps it's because we can't avoid each other, but if you need help family's the first place you go. This is why I suppose Nan and Auntie Julie and Auntie Susan and everybody are suspicious about Stuart. We're all pretty puzzled by him not visiting his family. It makes us think there's something not quite right about him.

I need to stop thinking about all this. I've felt anxious and nervous ever since I got back from school and I don't even know why. It's just so unlike me. I'm going to find Jack and Rascal. One of them is bound to want to come out for a walk.

7:05 p.m.

I went to the park with Jack and Rascal. Big mistake. I saw Loops there with Thomas Finch, in the teenagers' shelter. Not kissing, just chatting away. They waved and I waved back, and then dragged poor puzzled Jack and Rascal straight back home. Hideous. Consoled myself by buying me and Jack a big bag of chips.

I *knew* she'd get him in that shelter. It was only a matter of time.

10:15 p.m.

It's getting late now and I've realized there are two reasons why I am feeling strange. The first is that for the first time in years and years I'm not at Hannah's house. I'm sitting in Mum's bedroom writing this and listening to the Clones screaming in our room about the boys they like.

Hannah and Neil Parkhouse will—right now—be on their way back from Oxford and their first "proper date." I hope it went well. Hannah is so the type to have a steady boyfriend and then end up marrying him.

That means Loops and Thomas will have been alone together all evening. And if they were already in the teen-agers' shelter hours ago, who knows what they've been get-ting up to?

The second reason I feel odd is that tomorrow is the big day—the day of the Cunning Plan. We thought the whole thing up just a few weeks ago, but it seems like we've been waiting to do it forever.

After Jack went to bed tonight, Mum and me watched *Hairspray*. It was *brilliant*. It's now in my top ten movies of all time. Official. We closed the door so we couldn't hear the Clones, then we snuggled up on the sofa and scarfed micro-wave popcorn.

"It's nice doing this," said Mum, "just the two of us. I hope we're always going to have evenings like this—even when I'm an old lady!"

It got me thinking about how maybe she's not changing that much. Perhaps she can still be like the old mum even if she's with Stuart. Has it been me all along, not wanting to get used to the new situation? But it's far too late to go down that road. Whatever I think, there's no going back now.

Saturday, October 31: 8:44 p.m.

⊚ CRYING MODE ⊚

Some Grown-Ups cry at anything. All it takes for some is a sad film, or the Dogs Shelter advertisement, and they cry so much they could fill a small bathtub.

Some models of Grown-Up secretly enjoy being in Crying Mode and they feel great when they've "had a good cry." Other models, however, only cry when something really upsetting or awful has happened.

It's all over. Mum is crying her heart out in her bedroom. I could not feel worse than I do right now.

I'd better start at the beginning. Auntie Julie came over as planned for morning coffee.

"When is Stuart getting here?" she asked.

"Oh, early afternoon," said Mum. "He's nervous about the party, meeting all the family again."

"He'll be *fine,*" soothed Auntie Julie, "but listen, I've had this wonderful idea. Well, Mandy and Katie thought of it too."

"What idea?" said Mum.

"Mandy wants to get you looking *fantastic* for the party," said Auntie Julie, as casually as she could, "so she's asked if the rest of us could keep Stuart busy this afternoon. I was thinking that I could take Stuart and Jack and Katie up to the University Parks for a walk along the river."

"I don't know...," said Mum. "I didn't think it would take me that long to get ready...."

"Go on, let me do this," coaxed Auntie Julie. "Mandy's got something fantastic planned for you and she wants it to be a surprise."

"All right," said Mum, who's obviously lost all her Intuitive Functions. "I suppose we've always enjoyed the getting-ready part."

It was arranged that Auntie Julie and me would whisk Stuart and Jack away after lunch so Mandy could begin to work her magic on Mum.

When he arrived, Stuart was as unenthusiastic as Mum about the Plan, but had to go along with it, as he had no choice. He was very quiet at lunchtime, as if he was preoccupied about something. This could, of course, have been the sardines and mozzarella on toast.

I should explain at this point that it was never Auntie Julie's intention to actually take me and Stuart and Jack to Oxford. We walked to Auntie Julie's house and got them in her car, and then Auntie Julie pretended it wouldn't start.

"Oh dear," she said, turning to Stuart, "and we can't fit in your car, can we? Oh well, we'll have to think of something else to keep us busy for an hour or so."

"But I wanted to feed the ducks!" said a crestfallen Jack. I felt terrible that we'd built up his hopes of getting out of Brindleton for a few hours.

Stuart patted Jack on the back. "Never mind, mate," he said, "we'll think of something else fun to do. How about a hike?"

"We can't do that," said Auntie Julie quickly. "I couldn't keep up on one of your hikes. I know, why don't you come and visit some of the family? You've not met Great-Grandma Peters, have you? Apparently, when she was a young girl, she looked *just like Alison*."

"I'm not sure that's a good idea . . . ," said Stuart, looking cornered. But he was up against Auntie Julie, so he didn't have a hope.

So—as proposed all along in the Cunning Plan—we took poor Stuart to Great-Grandma Peters's house, where he had a preview of what Mum could be like in fifty years—a tiny and aggressive woman who swears a lot and has a face like a walnut.

Great-Grandma Peters was watching a cooking show and was not impressed with some celebrity chef.

"Now, that's an unholy mess," she said. "I wouldn't feed it to the dog. What does he think he's doing? What a stupid idiot he is with that haircut! So, who are you, then?"

"This is Stuart, Mum's boyfriend," I said.

Great-Grandma Peters looked Stuart up and down with her beady little eyes.

"Not bad-looking," she said, "but he's not a patch on Mike. Mike was the love of Alison's life, you know. They started going out when they were Katie's age, just thirteen. Ah, she'll never find another the same. Can I offer you a cookie? Or would you prefer a custard cream?"

We knew we could rely on Great-Grandma Peters to say whatever came into her head—and that it would be completely tactless. It's not that she means to hurt people's feelings; she just tells it like it is.

Still, Stuart looked hurt when she said he was not a patch on our dad. No wonder he didn't feel like a custard cream.

We left Jack at Great-Grandma Peters's house to keep

her company (he was not *at all* pleased), then dragged Stuart over to Nan and Granddad Williams's house.

"Maybe that's enough visiting," he said hopefully. But Auntie Julie was marching on ahead, not listening to a word he was saying.

Granddad Williams was out at his garden, so we were at the mercy of Nan. We sat in her front "best" room, which is full of memorabilia of the Royal Family. Stuart stared at the collection of jubilee plates covering the walls and ornaments on every available surface.

Because Nan's a smoker, the house stinks of cigarette smoke. We hardly notice it since we're used to it, but Stuart started coughing as soon as we walked in.

"I love our Royal Family," said Nan Williams as she brought Stuart his second cup of tea of the afternoon, "particularly Queen Elizabeth. She is a wonderful woman. She's got a *sense of duty,* she has." She looked pointedly at Stuart when she said this. This was the first time she'd seen him since we'd told her that he never visited his parents, all part of the Cunning Plan.

"So you work in the minimart," said Stuart, between coughs. "That must be interesting."

"It keeps me busy," said Nan Williams, lighting a cigarette and sitting back in her chair. "As they say, 'The devil makes work for idle hands.' I clean too. They don't call them the *filthy rich* for nothing! Now, I've been meaning to ask you about something that has been troubling me."

"Fire away!" said Stuart.

"I've heard that you never go and see your poor parents from one Christmas to the next. Has there been some sort of a falling-out?"

"No," said Stuart, switching into Irritated Mode.

"You may *think* that's enough," said Nan Williams, "but it's not. You seem like a nice enough young man, but what sort of person has no time for their family?"

Stuart stood up.

"I think we'd better go," he said, frowning and not meeting Nan's eye. Which made him look shifty.

"Well, *maybe you should*," said Nan Williams, standing up and blowing an indignant puff of smoke right into his face.

When we got out of her house, Stuart said quite firmly, "Let's get back and see how your mum's doing."

"But . . . we *can't* go back yet," said Auntie Julie frantically, "they'll need longer to get ready. How about one more visit? Let's go to Susan and Dave's—they live just round the corner. We'll get you a beer. I think you could use one."

So, on the strength of a beer he probably felt he needed, Stuart was persuaded to go to Auntie Susan and Uncle Dave's house.

Auntie Julie kept encouraging all the Grown-Ups to drink wine and beer, and then, when they were relaxed and off guard, cleverly turned the conversation to my dad, Uncle Dave's little brother.

Of course Uncle Dave's eyes misted over, and he told a few stories about my dad growing up. And then Auntie Susan had a few things to say about Mum and Dad and how they met. And Stuart couldn't miss the giant wedding picture of Mum and Dad on the mantelpiece, where they looked so young and in love (with Mum's wedding flowers strategically placed in front of the bump that was to become Mandy).

As the beer and wine flowed, and the stories about Mum and Dad and the wider family were told, Stuart seemed to withdraw into himself. No wonder. None of the stories did anything except make him feel more and more like an outsider. Although he continued to smile and nod politely, his eyes looked really sort of *hurt*.

For the first time I looked at Stuart not as someone who was wanting to take our mum away from us, but as just another human being trying to get by in the world. A human being who could be happy or sad or angry or hopeful . . . or lonely.

Then I realized that I felt incredibly, enormously sorry for him. Almost as if I could cry. And that I felt absolutely terrible about what we were doing. But it was like being on a train that's going faster and faster and you can't get off. It was too late to stop it.

Saturday, October 31: Midnight

☺ DEVASTATED MODE ☺

This could also be called Destroyed Mode, because it's when your Grown-Up is so shocked and upset by something it is hard for them to function at all.

If your Grown-Up is in Devastated Mode then it affects everyone—everything is confused and mixed up—it is like a hurricane or something.

The best course of action when your Grown-Up is in Devastated Mode is to hang on in there. Nobody can stay in Devastated Mode forever—nobody could possibly have the energy. Life has to go on, even if it is changed forever.

Mum is back in a place we never wanted her to ever go back to. She's in Devastated Mode. Somewhere we can't reach her. And we're the reason she's there. It's all our fault.

After the afternoon of the Plan, we made our excuses and walked back to our house, with Stuart saying not one word. Auntie Julie tried to make some sort of conversation, but he didn't reply.

When we got in the house and were in the hall, we heard Mum saying to Mandy, "I can't *wait* to see Stuart's face!"

We trooped into the living room, where Mum was sitting on the couch, dressed up.

Mandy said, "*Ta-da!* What do you think?"

It had taken hours of effort and Mum looked every bit the punk rocker, with heavy black eyeliner, fake piercings, lots of giant fake tattoos (including one of a spider's web on her neck), back-combed crimped hair (with a black rinse through it), chains, dog collar and a black garbage bag held together with safety pins. She looked terrifying.

Stuart stared at her.

"Can I speak to you outside?" he said.

"Why?" said Mum.

He took her by the arm and they disappeared into the backyard for about half an hour. Auntie Julie, Mandy and me sat in the living room, looking at each other.

Auntie Julie was just putting the kettle on when they came in from the garden and walked through to the front hall. Mum was obviously shocked and upset, her black eyeliner was smudged and she had mascara-colored tear tracks down her face.

Being dumped is bad enough, but being dumped when

you are wearing a black garbage bag held together with safety pins must be particularly humiliating. You might as well just put yourself in the trash can and be done with it.

"I think it's for the best," we heard Stuart saying. "I'm sorry."

We heard the front door close and the rustling of the garbage bag as Mum trudged upstairs. Then we heard her bedroom door slam shut.

Mum didn't want to talk to any of us, not even Auntie Julie. At one point, when Auntie Julie was knocking on the bedroom door, I heard Mum shout, "Julie, just *go home.*"

Auntie Julie went off, looking upset. I shouldn't think she'll be getting cups of tea and chocolate cookies and sympathy off Mum for a while.

But Mum, as usual, couldn't stay angry for long. Soon we heard her crying—terrible big sobs muffled by her pillow.

"Well," said Mandy flatly, "I suppose that's mission accomplished."

There was a long silence.

"I'm going to get Jack," I said finally, putting my coat on. I had to get out of the house.

He and Great-Grandma Peters were watching *Doctor Who.*

"That young gentleman," said Great-Grandma Peters, pointing at the doctor with a custard cream, "can do surprising things with a screwdriver . . . which is just as well with these evil slimy green things with the teeth chasing him."

Mandy went to the party in the end. First she took Jack and dropped him at Auntie Susan's to share Matthew's babysitter—she had to get him away from Mum's heartbreaking sobs. I didn't feel like going. Even Hannah and Loops couldn't persuade me when they came meowing round in their cat costumes, full of the Halloween mood.

"But Ben Clayden's going to be there!" said Hannah. She still thinks I love him. If only she knew the truth.

I couldn't face going to the party. Hannah with Neil, Loops with Thomas and Jonathan Elliott (or Giraffe Tongue, as I now think of him) waiting to lunge. Anyway, I didn't want to leave Mum.

So I've spent the evening writing this and cuddling Rascal on the sofa and occasionally knocking on Mum's door and being asked if I'd please just leave her alone.

Where are my skills in operating Grown-Ups now? How on earth can I switch Mum out of this mode?

What *on earth* have we done?

Saturday, November 14

 ZOMBIE MODE

Zombie Mode is not where your Grown-Up's left arm falls off as they stagger through a graveyard. It is a particular malfunction where your Grown-Up's mind seems to be completely empty—this mode can be induced in most models by switching on the TV. Zombie Mode often follows on from Tired Mode or it can be a side effect of Sad or Depressed Mode. Do not expect to get much useful function out of your Grown-Up when they are in this mode. Think of it as if they are on standby. Expert mode-switching is required to reactivate Grown-Ups from Zombie Mode.

Try as we might, nothing has worked to switch Mum out of her misery. Mum has been in Zombie Mode for the last couple of weeks. We've ruined her life.

Having your life ruined tends to preoccupy you, especially when your one chance of happiness has been taken away by people who're supposed to love you.

Mum's gone back to how she was after Dad died, moping around the house and not bothering to brush her hair. She was off work for a week and even now that she's gone back, she's forgetting classes.

I think Stuart said something in the yard about everybody going on about our dad, because Mum's hardly talking to Auntie Julie, or Uncle Dave and Auntie Susan. When they call round she makes excuses and won't invite them in.

I should be glad that she's stopped cooking and we're having frozen dinners, which are at least edible in a chemical, cardboardish sort of a way. Yes, even a chemical cardboard taste is better than anything poor Mum could come up with. But I wish she would get off the sofa and cook something truly disgusting. It would mean she was enjoying herself again.

10:00 p.m.

I am a horrible person. Because it's not just Mum that I've hurt. I've done something terrible tonight. There's *no way* I am going to get one wink of sleep.

No wonder I've almost given up on this guide. Who am I to tell you about Grown-Ups when it's so obvious that I haven't got a clue about managing their lives, or even my own?

Mum is miserable, and I'm miserable because she's miserable. And none of my so-called expert techniques in operating a Grown-Up are working. Of course they're not. Because I'm rubbish. I'm not an expert at all. I'm a great big fake. I know nothing. Don't ever listen to me again.

This isn't an operating guide that will be of any use to you if you're trying to control your Grown-Up; Mandy was right—it's just a pathetic diary of my tragic life. You might as well stop reading, especially as now I've outdone myself. Things were bad, but now they are Officially Worse. I've gone and done something just as terrible as what I did to Mum. Something happened that should have been wonderful, but thanks to how it happened, it's really, *really* bad and *I don't know how I'm going to sort it out.*

Tonight, Hannah was out on a date with Neil Parkhouse, yet again. Tenpin bowling, apparently.

I assumed that Loops was seeing Thomas, and for some insane reason I went up to the park on my own. It was getting late, and if Mum had not been so unlike herself there is no way she'd have let me leave the house and go off in the dark.

I was feeling very angry for three reasons:

1) Obviously because Mum is a total mess.

2) It's my fault that Mum's a total mess.

3) Hannah and Loops have started going out with

Neil and Thomas every chance they can, leaving me with nobody to hang out with. They even did it last night.

"Can you come round to mine later tonight, like after nine-thirty?" said Hannah over the phone. "It's just that me and Loops are meeting the boys."

"Tell you what," I said quietly, "I won't bother coming at all."

"Katie, don't be like that!" Hannah complained. "Just because you don't want to go out with anyone doesn't mean *we* shouldn't."

So a couple of hours ago I marched up to the park, too fed up to care that I was out on my own in the dark. When I got there I sat on my own on the swings, brooding about how unfair my life is.

Then I got spooked. The moon, which had been shining enough to give reasonable light, disappeared behind some clouds. It was so dark, I could hardly see the other end of the park.

I heard a crunching noise. Then another. A twig snapped. My heart began to beat really fast.

"Hello?" I called out.

Now I was starting to freak out. It was too dark to know

if I was alone or if there was someone creeping up on me. I have never in my *whole life* felt so scared.

Slowly I got to my feet and walked to the edge of the park. Then I opened the gate and ran as fast as I could across the park, toward the street at the other side where there were streetlights and where I would feel safe.

Near the edge of the park, I ran straight into Thomas Finch.

I was so relieved to see a familiar face.

"What's happened?" he said.

"Nothing," I gasped, out of breath, "I'm fine. I just got a bit scared. . . ."

"It's okay," he said, putting his arm around me. "Let's get you home. You're shaking."

So we walked home, his arm around me all the way.

"I've made you late," I said, when we got to the front door. I looked up at him. "You're probably meeting Loops."

"Not really, not like that . . . ," he said. Then he paused as if he was wondering whether to tell me something.

"We're splitting up," he said.

My heart leaped in the air and did a special celebration dance. I wondered why Loops hadn't told me, but at that exact moment I didn't care.

"Oh," I said. Then I couldn't stop myself, I grinned up at him like an idiot. Which you'd have thought might have put him off, but it didn't.

He leaned down and kissed me.

Not some horrible Giraffe Tongue type kiss (or how I'd imagine a Giraffe Tongue kiss would be). It was gentle, sweet, warm and lovely, the kind that I wanted to go on forever.

I hadn't realized how much I'd wanted that kiss and for how long.

We were interrupted by the sound of footsteps approaching on the pavement. It was Leanne and Shannon.

"Well, well, well," said Leanne. "I wonder what your so-called friend Loops is going to say about this. *She's* waiting for him at the minimart and *you're* kissing his face off round here! Nice one, Katie!"

They walked on, cackling with delight.

"But . . . you said you'd broken up . . . ," I said, looking to Thomas for confirmation. He looked uncomfortable.

"I was on my way to do it now."

"I think you'd better go," I said.

"I'm going to tell her right now," he said, and started to walk away. I just shook my head, turned and went into the house, closing the door behind me. It's incredible how quickly you can go from feeling on top of the world to feeling miserable again.

I ran straight to my room to text Hannah and Loops, but then realized I'd left my mobile at Hannah's house and Mandy was out so I couldn't borrow hers. I phoned Hannah but her voice mail was on, so I left a message asking her to call me straightaway. I did the same to Loops's mobile, which was also on voice mail. They haven't called back yet.

I feel absolutely sick about what's happened and that I can't get hold of Loops.

I've wondered for so long what it would be like to have my first kiss, and now it's happened. And my first kiss has betrayed one of my two best friends in the whole world.

Tomorrow—first thing—I'm going to go straight over to Loops's house to explain everything.

Sunday, November 15: 2:01 p.m.

At nine o'clock I was rushing my breakfast, all dressed and ready to go to Loops's house. Then the doorbell rang.

I opened the door to find Hannah and Loops. Loops's eyes were red; she'd obviously been crying. My heart sank.

"You'd better come in," I said.

They came in and we all went up to the Cupboard. Hannah was looking at me as if she didn't know me. It was horrible.

"I'm glad you're here," I said. "I was about to come over to explain something that happened last night. . . ."

"You don't need to tell us anything," said Loops, in a shaky voice. "I got the picture last night from Leanne. Katie, how *could* you?"

"Thomas told me you'd split up. . . ."

"So you got stuck in the moment then, did you?" Hannah was indignant. "Did you not think for one moment about how Loops might be feeling? If someone who you liked dumped *you,* how would *you* feel?"

"I didn't know he was dumping you . . . ," I protested. "I got the idea that you'd both decided."

"You *got the idea*?" said Loops. "Well, thanks for making sure you were clear about what was going on! I thought you were my friend."

"But I am! I *am* your friend!" I shook my head. "I just got the wrong idea and then it just happened. . . ."

"Oh, forget it!" said Loops. "You *lied* to us! You let us think that you didn't like him and then the minute you got the chance you just grabbed him, behind my back! Do you *know* how sneaky that is? You made me look so stupid! You know, I thought that you might actually apologize, but it seems you don't think you did anything wrong. Look, I'll see you around."

"Loops!"

I looked pleadingly at Hannah, expecting her to say something to back me up, to say to Loops that I would never hurt her on purpose. But she looked at the floor.

When Loops turned and left, Hannah followed her.

"See you, Katie," she said sadly.

I stood there in shock, thinking that they are absolutely right to hate me for what I've done. I am quite possibly the worst person in the history of the universe.

I closed the front door and walked back into the living room. Mum was on the sofa. The breakfast dishes were uncleared. Mandy was nowhere to be seen, and Jack was on the computer. The TV wasn't on, but Mum was staring at it. I realized that my two best friends walking out on me had completely passed her by.

9:32 p.m.

I spent the rest of the afternoon crying under my duvet and Mum didn't even notice. Mandy came home and saw my attractively swollen face and went straight into Sympathy Mode, thank goodness. I don't think I could have stood it if she hadn't cared.

Mandy was shocked that Mum was so out of it she hadn't noticed what was going on. It's like she's given up— she doesn't care about doing the laundry or even getting in basic provisions so we don't starve.

So we called Auntie Susan, who came over and looked at Mum and told us that she will come back tomorrow to take Mum to the doctor's. This must be serious.

Sunday, December 6: 3:00 p.m.

DEPRESSED MODE

This is when Grown-Ups are miserable, gloomy, moping about and thinking sad thoughts but it's not just a passing thing, it goes on for ages. Think of Sad Mode but going on and on and on.

Sometimes there's a good reason for a Grown-Up to be in Depressed Mode; sometimes there's no reason at all. Some say it's a chemical thing in the brain. It's definitely an illness and so there is only one piece of good advice: get your Grown-Up to see a doctor.

Mum saw the doctor almost three weeks ago. She's on antidepressants and I'm hoping they'll start to help soon. It can take a while, apparently.

Mum spends a lot of time on the sofa, watching but not watching the TV. Every time I see her looking small and sad I feel terrible for what we've done. She must know we were behind it, but she hasn't said anything. She's not angry at Mandy and me. She's in Depressed Mode. Which is, of course, far worse.

{274}

As if that's not bad enough, Hannah and Loops haven't spoken to me since they told me what they thought of me. And I haven't had the heart to write about it. Or to write anything, in fact . . .

Because I don't have Hannah or Loops, Leanne has been giving me a hard time every chance she gets. She's been following me around saying I have no friends and everyone hates me. The Mutants follow her as she follows me, laughing at everything she says.

"Thomas Finch said you're a terrible kisser," she'll say. "He said it was like kissing a fish."

"I don't care," I say.

But I do.

I know she's lying, because even if it were true, how would Thomas know how a fish kisses? Imagine if that was how he'd learned. That would definitely be worse than Hannah practicing on her hand.

Thomas tried to talk to me. He came up to me on the school bus.

"I'm sorry," he said.

"Forget it," I said, "it was my own stupid fault for believing what you said. I'd like you to stay away from me, please."

I'm angry with him for misleading me and for what he did to Loops. Of course Neil Parkhouse and Jonathan Elliott are still buddies with him. If you're a boy, you can get away with anything and your mates will still think you're the best thing since sliced bread. Meanwhile, I'm the Outcast.

To be fair, Hannah and Loops are not being mean to me—probably because they see that Leanne has that taken care of. They just act like I'm invisible.

I'm too embarrassed and ashamed of myself to try to talk to them, so it's not like I'm trying and they're ignoring me . . . but when I walk past they don't look at me.

Auntie Susan and Auntie Julie have been coming over most days to help us out and to try to get Mum interested in things.

"She's just like she was after Mike died," said Auntie Susan, in the kitchen.

"No," said Auntie Julie, "I think she's worse."

Auntie Susan's in Worried Mode because Hannah and me are not talking.

"I don't know what caused this, but can't you two just get over it?" she asked me.

"You *don't understand*," I said.

7:42 p.m.

You know how they say "misery loves company"? Well, Mandy and me are getting along famously now that we are both feeling so terrible. There hasn't been any shouting or arguments for weeks.

Actually, Mandy's being great. I told her what happened with Hannah and Loops, so she's being quite protective. She sits beside me instead of the Clones on the school bus. Which is just about the nicest thing she's ever done for me.

Thank goodness Jack has the thick skin of a rhinoceros. I think he's actually enjoying that we all have less to say. Now he can tell us all about his favorite *Doctor Who* characters for hours on end and we won't interrupt.

The other day he burped the entire national anthem. Note perfect. Even that could not cheer me up.

But he's not a complete rhinoceros.

"When's Stuart coming back?" he says now and again. He said it today.

I said to Mandy the other night, when we were going to sleep, "We shouldn't have done it, should we?"

There was this long silence. Then she answered in a very small, very unlike-Mandy sort of voice, "No."

BRAVE FACE MODE

Many models of Grown-Ups are very good at Brave Face Mode, where they put on a cheerful appearance with other people, when really they are a quivering wreck who—in the privacy of their own home—can hardly move from the sofa.

It can be useful if your Grown-Up can go into Brave Face Mode because it saves embarrassment when you are out with them. It's not much fun having your Grown-Up bursting into tears in the post office and telling some stranger in line all their troubles.

However, some models of Grown-Ups are so good at Brave Face Mode, other Grown-Ups don't realize they need help. In such a case it's up to you to let the right people know.

It's only a week till school breaks up for Christmas and it's nearly a whole month since I fell out with Hannah and Loops. It's been pretty hideous, but I think that after all I've done I deserve to be miserable. Betraying one of your best friends, breaking your mum's heart . . . I'm a class act.

The antidepressants are working. Mum's getting up and doing things now. She's putting a brave face on things because of Christmas coming, so she's even pretending to be enthusiastic about putting up the decorations.

But despite Mum walking and talking and seeming normal again, I can't operate her anymore. I can't reach her. It's as if there is a bubble around her. If you didn't know her, you wouldn't know there was anything wrong, but we can see it.

She is just not herself.

She doesn't do all the silly little things she used to do, like laughing uncontrollably at something stupid on TV (like a dog wearing a hat or something) or telling us we look "ravishing" when we're just in our school uniforms or announcing out of nowhere that beards should be against the law.

She doesn't even do her Saturday-morning puttering-about in Dad's clothing anymore.

In the evenings, when Jack's gone to bed, we all sit together and watch TV, huddled up together on the sofa. The other week there was a dog on a skateboard wearing sunglasses—Mum didn't even crack a smile.

Mandy and me aren't going out for sleepovers or seeing anyone. Well, I don't have a choice, if I'm honest, seeing as I have no friends now. But even if I did, I don't think I'd want to leave Mum when—despite her brave face—I know she's not herself. Mandy feels the same way. After all, what happened is completely our fault.

Even Rascal is depressed. He's pining for Stuart! He won't sit on the sofa with us anymore, but sits under the kitchen table looking very put out.

I wish things could go back to how they were before.

Monday, December 14: 9:30 p.m.

Mum had an evening training session with Mrs. Caulfield, so Auntie Julie came over to see us.

"Do you think she's getting better?" she asked. "Is she over him yet?"

"It looks like she's *never* going to be over him," said Mandy. "She's going to be sad and lonely for the rest of her life."

"So what should we do?" I said to Auntie Julie. "You thought of the Cunning Plan. I can't get through to her. Nothing is working. Can you think of a way that we could get them back together?"

Auntie Julie looked at me as if I was mad.

"Get them *back together?*" said Auntie Julie. "Why would we want to do that? Isn't this what you said you wanted? Give her a few months and I'll take her speed dating in Oxford and she'll have hundreds of men falling over themselves to go out with her."

"So *that's* what it's all about," I said, realization dawning.

"What?" Auntie Julie looked uncomfortable.

"You just want someone to go speed dating with, so you don't have to do it on your own!"

"That's *not true*!" she said, looking very uncomfortable. "Well, maybe it is . . . but don't try to pin this all on me. It was you two who talked me into helping. It was *you* who wanted to get rid of him. I only want what's best for your mum."

"No you don't!" I shouted.

☹ SAD BUT TRUE FACT

Grown-Ups can be just as self-deluding, childish and selfish as we are. Get used to it.

I ran out of the house and down the street, not knowing where I was going, but needing to run because I was so angry with Auntie Julie—and with myself.

After about a hundred meters, of course, I bumped into a relative. Statistically, this was bound to happen. It happened to be Nan. I almost knocked the cigarette out of her hand.

"What's *wrong* with you?" she said. "Every time I see you these days you look like it's the end of the world."

"Nothing," I said, still feeling angry. "Anyway, I can't

tell *you*, can I? Anything I tell you gets round the whole village. I might as well phone the local radio station."

Nan looked wounded. "Is that what you think? That I can't keep a secret? Well, I'll have you know that I know secrets that would make your hair curl. If anyone tells me something in confidence, then it stays that way. 'Loose lips sink ships!'—that's what they said in the war. You can go on your way if you want, but if you want to come with me and have a cup of tea and tell your nan all about it, I can promise you that it will go no further."

So I went to Nan's and I had a cup of tea out of one of her Golden Jubilee mugs. I told her everything. About the Cunning Plan and Stuart leaving and Mum being broken-hearted. I told her about falling out with Hannah and Loops over Thomas. But I didn't tell her about Mandy and Joshua Weston. That's Mandy's business.

"Well, that's quite a tale," she said when I'd finished. "So what are you going to do? 'Where there's a will, there's a way.'"

"I don't know," I said. "I don't know what to do. I've thought about telling Mum, or phoning Stuart, or even going up to Oxford to talk to him. Then I think I've done enough already."

Nan went into her kitchen to wash up our mugs, then came back and sat down and took a deep breath.

"I agree. I think you should do nothing."

"Nothing?"

"That's what I said. Absolutely *nothing*. Your mum lost your father, and he was her rock. What she needs—and what you all need—is the next person in your lives to be someone who'll stick around, not run at the first sign of trouble. If Stuart loves her the way she deserves to be loved, he shouldn't care about what you or any of us think. What you did with your silly plan was like a test, and in my opinion he failed it."

I hadn't thought of it like that. It made me feel better.

"Thanks, Nan," I said.

"And one more thing," she said, "I think it's about time you went and apologized to your friends. 'It's never too late to mend.'"

Tuesday, December 15: 9:40 p.m.

Today I summoned up more courage than I've ever needed in my life before. After school I went to Loops's house.

Joshua answered the door.

"I don't think she wants to see you," he said with his usual scowl (which makes it hard to know if he is annoyed or just being his normal self).

"Please," I begged.

Loops appeared behind him. "It's okay," she said, "she can come in."

She showed me through to her bedroom, where Hannah was sitting on the bed. Neither of them would look me in the eye.

I wondered if Hannah was going to have a sleepover at Loops's house, the way I used to at hers. I felt like I'd been cheated on, which is stupid. I've got to realize that some things change and if Hannah and me don't have our sacred Friday nights anymore it doesn't mean we're not still best friends.

I took a deep breath.

"I've come to say I'm sorry. I don't deserve to be your friend . . . and I miss you. I miss both of you *so much*."

Then I couldn't go on; I started to cry. It all came rushing out, all the sadness I'd been feeling seeing Mum so miserable and missing Hannah and Loops and messing everything up. I stood in the doorway of the room and blubbed like a baby.

Which was when I found out what brilliant friends I have. Because they instantly went into Hugging Mode, and there's nothing like Hugging Mode to make everything a million, billion, zillion, trillion times better.

After we'd hugged for ages and cried some more, Loops got chocolate out of the secret stash she keeps under her bed. And we got down to the serious business of catching up.

"Guess who Loops is seeing?" said Hannah, grinning.

"Who?" I said, and for a moment I wondered if it was Thomas Finch. I told myself that if it was then I had to just accept it. There's always the Himalayas.

"Jonathan Elliott!" shrieked Loops.

I was surprised at how relieved I felt.

"It's all because I found out Ailsa Prior likes him!"

Ailsa Prior is good-looking, sophisticated and cool—and she's *sixteen*. Loads of boys fancy her. But I couldn't understand what Loops was going on about.

"I found out she had a thing for Jonathan!" explained Loops. "I heard Mandy talking to Lucy Parrish about it on the bus last week. That's when I realized that I still liked him, because I didn't want him to go out with her, I wanted him to go out with *me*! So I went and asked him . . . and that was that!"

"*And* he told Loops that he prefers *her*!" said Hannah, totally delighted for Loops.

"Jonathan says he has a thing for redheads," said Loops smugly. "Did you know that only two percent of the world's population has red hair and we might be *extinct* in less than a hundred years?"

I could guess who'd told her that fascinating fact. It turns out she's always preferred Jonathan.

"I liked Thomas," Loops said, "but there was never that spark like there is with Jonathan. You know, I think Thomas has always liked *you*, Katie."

"Well, that's not going to happen," I said.

Loops smiled and put her arm around me. "If it did happen," she said, "I wouldn't mind."

I walked home with a giant smile on my face. I think that tonight I'm going to sleep better than I have in weeks.

But I mean it about Thomas Finch. The moment has passed.

Friday, December 18: 7:10 p.m.

DETERMINED MODE

When a Grown-Up goes into Determined Mode they really want to achieve something. It is best to be supportive of your Grown-Up when they are like this, as they will focus on their goal and move toward it single-mindedly, and they will not let anything get in their way.

You know, it's funny how things work out. I mean, Mum's now on proper good terms with Auntie Julie and Uncle Dave and Auntie Susan again and we're having them all over on Christmas Eve for dinner.

Despite everything that happened and their part in it, she's never going to turn her back on them—family's too important to her.

Mum is in full Determined Mode about making this dinner party a success. And I am not going to try to talk her out of it. I'm just relieved that she has some enthusiasm again—even if it is does mean poisoning us all.

"I'll cook you all something *really special*," she said to Auntie Susan and Uncle Dave, when we were at their house on Sunday. They tried to look delighted—all except Matthew, who looked frightened. He's obviously afraid he might lose his taste buds like Jack has.

Even better, school finished for Christmas today. Yee-ha! And it ended *spectacularly*.

Leanne and Shannon and the Mutants found me at lunchtime on the playground, and Leanne started taunting me as usual.

"Look, it's little Miss No-Mates," she started.

As usual, I ignored them. I wondered what would come next. Maybe a taunt about my knobbly knees.

I tried to walk off, but Leanne cornered me and squirted some water from her water bottle over my head.

"Sorry!" Leanne said. "I keep *accidentally* spilling water all over you!"

I tried to brush the water out of my eyes, but Leanne kept squirting me. My hair was sopping wet and dripping. Then I saw Hannah and Loops come running over. Hannah knocked the water bottle out of Leanne's hand and Loops kicked it across the playground. Then they stood beside me, shoulder to shoulder.

"Leave her alone," Loops said firmly.

You should have seen Leanne's face.

"So what else are you going to do to me, Leanne?" I said. "I seem to have found some mates after all."

She gave her nasty little smile. You could see her tiny brain working out that there were still only three of us and she had Shannon and all the Mutants on her side.

I was beginning to regret my big mouth, when Mandy came charging over with the Clones.

"Is there a problem?" said Mandy. Now they were standing with us side by side against Leanne and the Mutants. It was the *best* feeling.

"Oh, she's been joined by *all* her **LOSER** friends," shouted Leanne. The Mutants laughed like robots.

There were still more of them than of us, and it occurred to me that if it turned into a huge girl fight, we might not do so well.

It was then that Joshua Weston arrived, scowling, with Harry and Jake and about three other friends in tow—two of them were great big tall lads.

"Are you calling my sister a loser?" Joshua said to Leanne. "Because if you are, say it to me first."

He turned to me. "Next time these idiots bother you, give us a shout, okay?"

I nodded. I could have kissed him, and Jake, and Harry.

It had to be one of the top moments of my life so far, seeing Leanne's face right then. There's nobody more cowardly than a bully.

Leanne and the Mutants slunk off, like the hyenas in *The Lion King*.

"You all right, Mandy?" Joshua Weston turned and smiled at Mandy.

"Er . . . yeah!" she said, blushing absolutely crimson. She was so lost for words she couldn't even come up with an insult.

8:10 p.m.

I went to see Great-Grandma Peters on the way home—since we got out early. She was watching a DIY show.

"Look at the state of that living room!" she was saying. "And they call it a makeover! More like an instant headache. Just look at that wallpaper! So how's your mum? Is she still seeing that handsome young man?"

"No, Gran, she's not," I said.

"Pity," she said, "he had very strong-looking forearms."

When I got home, Loops rang and told me that Joshua Weston has split up with Jenny Caulfield, so I *immediately* told Mandy. She pretended not to be bothered, but

I could see she was mega-happy about it. I am so pleased for her!

9:30 p.m.

Mandy is still smiling to herself. And even Mum is looking almost cheerful. She is sitting on the sofa surrounded by recipe books, planning the Christmas Eve menu. This is the most motivated I've seen her since Stuart left. Maybe, just maybe, things are going to be okay.

One of Dad's favorite sayings when he was in Wise Mode was "It's not what happens to you in life that says who you are, it's how you react to what life throws at you."

Despite everything that's happened to her, despite what we've done, Mum has picked herself back up and is getting on with it. She's in Determined Mode, and I know nothing's going to get in her way.

I think Dad would be very proud of Mum right now. I know I am.

Christmas Eve: 5:00 p.m.

SHOPPING MODE ⊚

There are two types of Shopping Mode—"get it over with" Shopping Mode and "fun" Shopping Mode. Most male models of Grown-Ups tend to only function in "get it over with" Shopping Mode, especially if they are Christmas shopping for their wife or girlfriend.

A completely different type of Shopping Mode is Bargain Hunting—just hope that your Grown-Up does not go into this type of Shopping Mode or before you know it you'll be going round endless yard sales with them, or fending for yourself while they spend eighteen hours at a time on eBay.

Mum's in the kitchen cooking dinner for tonight and probably trying to keep her mind off what happened this afternoon in Oxford. We went up for some last-minute Christmas shopping.

Mum's usually a "get it over with" shopper—when it comes to buying milk and bread at the Brindleton minimart, that is. But today in Oxford she was in full-on "fun" Shopping Mode.

We went to loads of shops and she was interested in

everything—giving us advice about what to get and giving us all some extra cash, saying, "Don't spend it all in the same shop!"

We went into one shop full of Christmas stuff—like decorations and joke presents. Mum loved it. It was good to see her so upbeat. She seemed to get a huge amount of pleasure out of trying on some joke reindeer antlers made of stuffed velvet with bells on.

"What do you think?" she asked, shaking her head so that the bells tinkled.

"You look fantastic," I said, which was a bit of a White Lie, because she didn't, she looked ridiculous. But I couldn't bring myself to spoil her fun and neither could Mandy or Jack, who also told her she looked great.

Big mistake.

Mum not only bought herself a pair . . . *she wore them out of the shop*. Which is Brave Face Mode gone way too far, in my opinion.

Worse still, she continued to wear them when we went for a pizza. So when we sat down I was not surprised to see that Ben Clayden and his family were sitting three tables away from us. Of *course* he was there! He's always around when something embarrassing is happening to me.

When I was actually in control of Mum, I would have

been able to do something clever to get her to take the antlers off in five seconds flat. But I was so out of practice, I couldn't think of anything!

I sneaked a glance from behind the giant laminated menu over at Ben Clayden, who was tucking into a pepperoni pizza. In a few seconds he'd be sure to notice us. Then something struck me. And this, for me, is *huge*.

I realized that despite Mum looking totally tragic and me having to be seen with her, *I didn't want her to take the antlers off.* I realized that for once I didn't care what Ben Clayden or anyone else thought. Wearing the reindeer antlers was making her happy. That was all that mattered.

So I ordered garlic bread and a salad and when Ben Clayden did look over and see us, I waved and gave him a big smile. And I realized something else. I was breathing normally. I felt fine—I felt hardly anything, in fact. I don't want to have Ben Clayden's children anymore!! I can't wait to tell Hannah. She'll be amazed.

After lunch, we went to the University Parks and walked along by the river—it was where we said we were going to go with Stuart the day of the Cunning Plan. Just going there made me feel incredibly guilty.

We were all bundled up in our scarves and woolly hats,

hoping it might snow, and then the funniest thing happened. We bumped into Auntie Julie, who was obviously on one of her blind dates.

The man she was with was wearing a big fur hat, an old-fashioned suit and a long black velvet cloak fastened at the neck with some sort of bejeweled brooch. He looked like a character from one of those period dramas on TV that Mum likes. He was holding Auntie Julie's arm with one hand, and in his other hand was a silver-topped cane! He was at least seventy, with a giant white bushy beard.

"Hello!" Auntie Julie said nervously. "Hector, this is my sister and her children. Alison, this is Hector. He's a lecturer at Oxford University."

"Auntie Julie," said Jack, "why are you on a date with Santa Claus? Isn't he about a thousand years old?"

I deliberately didn't look at Mandy or I'd have cracked up. Jack opened his mouth ready to say something else, probably worse.

"Well, it's a pity but we really have to rush. See you later, Julie," said Mum hurriedly, grabbing Jack and walking briskly on.

"You know," Mum said, as we walked away, shaking her antlers in wonder, "I always thought that Julie was *exaggerating* when she told me about her blind dates."

"Let's go to the Westgate Center," said Mandy. "There's people there wrapping Christmas presents for charity."

"Only if the line's not too long," said Mum.

The charity Christmas present wrappers were sitting at a long table, wearing Santa hats and wrapping piles of presents in return for donations.

"I'm going to get them to wrap all my presents and then give them ten pence," we heard a bloke in front of us boast. He had a mean, weasel-like face.

"I think there's a minimum donation," said his mate knowledgeably. "They've got to cover the cost of the paper."

"Well, I'll give the minimum," said the man. *Nothing like getting in the Christmas spirit,* I thought.

It was then that I spotted Stuart. He was the third Santa-hat-wearing person along. He was busy wrapping a bubble-bath set for an old lady, curling ribbon like an expert and managing to flirt with her at the same time.

I was quite shocked to see him. As I watched him being kind to the old lady, I thought that if Mum had to go out with someone, Stuart wasn't that bad. He's *never* been that bad. Imagine if she brought home that horrible weasel-faced man who wanted to give the charity ten pence? It would serve us right if she did.

Mum dug her fingers into my arm, which meant she'd seen Stuart too.

"Let's go!" she said, pulling her antlers off with her other hand.

"Ow!" I protested.

"Go? Why?" said Mandy. "We're near the front!"

At this point Jack saw Stuart and began to jump up and down in his usual mad-frog way, waving madly.

"Stuart! Stuart!"

"We're *going*!" said Mum, just as Stuart saw us. The happy expression on his face disappeared instantly.

Mum grabbed Jack's hand and we all began to walk away, with Jack shouting, "But I want to see Stuart!"

As we made our way through the crowd, I looked round and saw that Stuart had stood up and was craning his neck to try to spot us.

He didn't come after us, though. He probably couldn't abandon his old lady with her bubble bath half wrapped. Or they'd have taken his Santa hat away.

You know, if life was like a Hollywood film, he'd have come running after us, knocking people's shopping bags flying. But life's not like it is in the movies, is it?

Christmas Eve: 10:11 p.m.

DELIRIOUS MODE

Delirious Mode is like Happy Mode, but the happy feelings are multiplied by about a thousand. It does not happen often and can lead to Reckless Mode—so make sure you keep a close watch on your Grown-Up in such circumstances.

I can't believe I'm saying this, but Mum is happy—more than happy. She's fantastically, brilliantly ecstatic and it's nothing to do with me! And I don't care!

That's why this is probably almost the last entry in this User's Guide; after this what can I say? I mean, I've realized that if you completely ignore my advice you'd probably be making the best decision. I doubt this will ever get published. If it did, I might get sued for pretending I am an expert.

Here's what happened.

Auntie Julie, Auntie Susan and Uncle Dave arrived with Hannah and Matthew at about six o'clock. The expression on their faces when we opened the door and the cooking smell hit their nostrils was hilarious. I wish I'd had the camera handy to capture the look of complete horror.

Auntie Julie rushed into the kitchen,

"I *so* need a drink!" she gasped. "That . . . *man*! He said in his personal ad that he was in his *forties*! I wasn't expecting a senior citizen!"

Mum poured her a large glass of wine.

"Speaking of *older* people," Mum said, "Mum and Dad are coming too."

At that moment, the doorbell rang and there were Nan and Granddad Williams. Granddad was brandishing a turnip triumphantly, for no particular reason.

"What do you think of *this,* then?" he said by way of hello.

I think old people's sense of smell is not so good, as they didn't seem too upset by the strange odors wafting through from the kitchen.

"Sit down at the table, everyone," said Mum. "This is a proper dinner party!"

You could see she was making a big effort to show everyone she was okay, still in Brave Face and Determined modes, but her happy act didn't fool me. Her mouth was smiling and she was saying all the right, cheery things. But her eyes were still sad.

We don't have the biggest house and we don't have a proper dining room, so Mum had rigged up the kitchen table together with another folding table to make one big table in the lounge.

The sofa was pushed against the wall to make room, so we had to climb over one another to get to our seats, which were all of different types and heights. I was in an office chair that's usually used for the computer.

When we all had managed to sit down and everyone had their drinks, Mum came through with the appetizer.

"Have you ever tried jellied eel bruschetta?" she inquired.

I do not know how we all did it, but we actually managed to eat that starter. I am certain that it will stay in our memories for many years to come. Nan had brought a couple of bottles of vintage Cava, which soon disappeared.

"It seems to help get rid of the taste," whispered Auntie Julie as she poured herself a third glass.

Not being allowed to drink, I had to resort to running upstairs and swilling my mouth out with mint mouthwash.

I'd just got back down and was preparing myself mentally for the main course when the doorbell rang. Auntie Susan answered it.

"Oh! What a surprise!" we heard her say, and then Stuart was standing in the room. Rascal flew at him like a little, white, furry guided missile and started leaping up at him madly, yelping with joy and excitement. It was like he was a puppy again.

In the middle of the commotion, Mum emerged from the kitchen holding a casserole dish.

"Stuart!" she cried, and then she carefully put the dish down on the table. I had secretly hoped, since it was a moment of great emotion, that she might drop it. No such luck.

Stuart looked around the room at us all.

"I've got something to say," he said, "and I need you all to listen. Apart from Jack, here, most of you have made it very clear that you don't want me in your family, so I walked away.

"I thought it was unfair to Alison for her to be stuck in the middle. But I've had time to think about things, and do you know what? If I have to put up with you lot to be with Alison, then I'll just have to. I'll put up with everything you throw at me."

He looked at Mum then.

"I love you. I've loved you since the moment I met you. If you still want me, I'm yours. But from now on I've got to be honest with you. If I don't say this now I might never say it and it has to be said. You are the *worst* cook I've ever met.

You have no idea how terrible you are . . . you are so, so *bad* at it!"

At this point, Mum sat down in her chair, put her face in her hands and burst into tears.

"It's all right," said Auntie Julie, patting Mum's shoulder and glaring at Stuart, "he's just leaving."

Mum looked up, puffy-eyed. Her nose was red. *Not* attractive.

"But I don't want him to go," she wailed. "I want him to stay!"

Stuart did not seem to mind Mum's mutant puffy-eyed, Rudolph-the-Red-Nosed-Reindeer look (which was very convincing, seeing as she was wearing her comedy antlers). He was gazing at her adoringly.

"What *I* want to know," said Nan, who was slightly under the influence of the vintage Cava, "is why you're here, upsetting my daughter, instead of spending Christmas with your own family. Or doesn't family mean much to you?"

Stuart looked at the ceiling in despair, exactly like a teacher would when a pupil says or does something spectacularly stupid. Funnily enough, I know that look well.

Before he could say anything, Mum got to her feet.

"Do you mind?" she said, looking at Stuart.

"It's okay," he said, "you can tell them."

Mum cleared her throat.

"Stuart was taken into foster care when he was six. He went to his final set of foster parents when he was sixteen and he was only with them for a short time. *They're* the parents he sees a couple of times a year."

We all looked at Stuart, whose face had reddened. I could see that this was hard for him. At last he spoke.

"I've spent years never feeling like I ever belonged anywhere. My foster parents, the last ones I had, helped me make something of myself. But while they're fantastic friends and I'll always be grateful to them, they're not family. I have no family.

"When I met Alison, I got to know all of you and saw how much you all looked out for each other—even if you drove each other mad. I felt that I was looking in at something special."

Then he looked directly at Nan, who was—perhaps for the first time in her life—looking shamefaced.

"You can say a lot of things about me and you'd probably be right, but don't *ever* tell me I don't care about family. Believe it or not, I care a lot about yours."

There was a long silence.

Uncle Dave stood up.

"I'll get us another chair from upstairs—why don't you take this one, mate?"

Stuart sat down. Mum, who was looking happier than I've ever seen her, lifted the lid on the casserole dish. An indescribably foul stink swept across the table.

"I can't believe you're saying I can't cook," she said defiantly as she stirred the unidentifiable mixture with the serving spoon. "Everyone *loves* my cooking!"

Mandy, who was sitting beside Mum, put her arm around her.

"Listen, there's something we've all been meaning to tell you. . . ."

Half an hour later, the pizzas arrived.

CHRISTMAS EVE: MUCH LATER

Later on, Jack disappeared, then rushed back into the room, shouting that it was snowing! We all rushed outside and stood in wonder in the garden.

No matter how many times it happens, snow always takes you by surprise. There's something magical about it. And this was the perfect snow, great big flakes falling slowly and settling on the ground. It was already several centimeters deep. It must have been falling silently for an hour or so.

We stood enjoying it, Jack dancing about like a little mad elf. Even Mandy was smiling.

I saw that Stuart had his arm around Mum and she was snuggled into his side. I felt a little tug of sadness that it was Stuart and not Dad, but at least she was happy.

It seemed as good a moment as any, so I went up to her.

"Can I talk to you for a second?" I said.

"Of course!" she said, disentangling herself from Stuart. We walked away from the others, her arm around my shoulder.

"I wanted to say how sorry I am," I said, "for how I've been. I'm going to make more of an effort . . . you know . . . with Stuart and stuff."

"Katie, that's the *best* Christmas present you could give me!" said Mum, beaming from ear to ear and giving me a huge hug. Stuart was watching us and he smiled this broad smile because he could see that what I'd said had made her happy. And if that's what he wants most of all, for Mum to be in Happy Mode—it's okay by me.

We could hear shouting and snow-muffled footsteps out on the street, and then the doorbell rang. It was Loops. She was wearing about six scarves, gloves and a woolly hat, which perched at a rakish angle on her crazy curls.

"Snowball fight at the park!" she cried, breathless with excitement. That's one thing about living in a village like Brindleton. We're excellent at making our own entertainment.

Hannah, Jack and me bundled into our jackets and coats and hats and followed Loops down the road. There were already loads of kids there, pelting each other with snowballs.

Neil Parkhouse ran up and stuffed a snowball down Hannah's coat. She screamed her head off, then chased him toward the park. Loops and me got stuck in the middle of it and we got hit more than we hit other people.

Then Jonathan came up. I began to feel like an outsider as he and Loops threw snowballs playfully at each other.

"Did you know," said Jonathan, "that it's a myth that it can be too cold to snow? Although it has to be said that most snowfalls occur when the air is warmer than minus nine degrees Celsius."

"He's so *clever!*" whispered Loops proudly. "He knows *everything!*"

She threw a huge snowball at him and ran off laughing. Jonathan stopped his snow lecture and did something far more intelligent—he chased Loops.

Leaving me standing alone. Which didn't bother me. I mean, it's something I've got used to recently. A whole month of having no mates was the worst time of my life, but it made me realize a few things about myself. Which is no bad thing. I've realized that I don't know all the answers. And how you treat people is—like my dad said—the most important thing. Love is all we need.

Then I realized I wasn't alone anymore. Thomas Finch was standing beside me, not saying anything. *No change there,* I thought.

He kept standing there. Not one single word.

"Hi," I said at last, and smiled at him. It was Christmas Eve. It was snowing. I couldn't carry on being angry with him forever.

He smiled back, that fantastic shy smile of his. Then he reached into his pocket and brought out a little parcel clumsily wrapped in Christmas paper. He practically threw it at me.

"You got me a *present*?" I said, surprised. "Shall I open it now?"

He shrugged, massively embarrassed, of course. I tore off the paper. There was a small box, and inside that was the most beautiful ruby-red glass heart key ring.

It was then that I finally understood why Thomas can talk to Loops but finds it so hard to talk to me. The glass shone in my hand.

"Thank you for my present," I said. Then I stood on tip-toe and kissed him. And he kissed me right back. Which is just about the best thing that's happened to me all year.

Christmas Eve: Later Still

 PHILOSOPHICAL MODE

Philosophical Mode is when Grown-Ups ask big questions about the universe, such as "Why are we here?" or "Do animals have souls?" or "Where did I put my car keys?"

Philosophical Mode can often accompany Midlife Crisis Mode. Try to discourage this sort of behavior in your Grown-Up, as it has a high Embarrassment Factor.

I've got the feeling that Stuart is going to be one of those Grown-Ups who goes into Philosophical Mode and generally thinks too much. I can see the signs already. There's his concern about the environment and the future of mankind for one thing.

I'll definitely have to bear this in mind if I'm going to master operating him. He's far too deep for his own good. It's lucky he's got shallow old me to sort him out. That yellow knitted tie's got to go, for starters.

It's going to be Christmas Day in a few hours, and it's going to be a good one. For one thing, I'm going to get that new cell phone I've had my eye on.

And better still, now that Mum's hung up her apron, Mandy and I are planning to cook the turkey by *following a recipe in a book*. I don't know how we'll do, but let's face it, things can only get better.

Mum and Stuart are upstairs in Mum's room, talking. They've got a lot of catching up to do.

Jack's tucked up in bed, with his enormous Christmas stocking laid out for Santa Claus to fill with presents. Mandy is watching TV and cuddling Rascal, who is looking extremely handsome with gold tinsel round his collar.

And I'm curled up writing this, feeling pretty philosophical myself.

I've no idea what the future holds for Mum and Stuart, or for any of us.

I don't know if Auntie Julie's ever going to find a boyfriend who isn't mad, or weird, or in his nineties.

I don't know if Nan will ever stop spreading the village gossip—though now I know she *can* keep a secret, if you ask her to.

I don't know if Jack will one day stop being enormously proud when he burps. I hope for his sake that this happens before he's forty.

I don't know if Mandy will ever tell Joshua Weston just how much she likes him.

And I don't know if a day will ever pass when I don't think about Dad.

There's only one thing I know for sure. Every ending is also a beginning. And do you know what? I like beginnings.

ONE LAST PIECE OF IMPORTANT ADVICE

Your Grown-Up is a complex and delicate piece of equipment, prone to much malfunction and error. Please handle your Grown-Up with care and caution.

One day, you yourself will become a Grown-Up. You may even have children of your own. If this happens, let's just hope that they find this guide in a dusty old drawer somewhere, before you get completely out of control.